The dizzying embrace continued and then, as if with infinite reluctance, his lips left hers and he relaxed, holding her gently now, letting her lean against him as the blood began to pound less rapidly in her veins. Briefly she felt the brush of his cheek against her hair, then he lifted his head and spoke to the girls behind her. She could feel the growing embarrassment in her own face.

'That's definitely adults only.' His voice sounded amused, but Jane could hear the rapid thud of his heart beneath her ear and had felt the fine tremor in the hand which had touched her hair. It was some comfort to know that he was almost as shaken as she had been by the kiss.

His expression was quizzical as he watched the colour rise in her face. 'You may not like to acknowledge it,' he challenged her, 'but you can't pretend a certain powerful chemistry isn't there.'

DANGEROUS ENGAGEMENT

BY

LYNN JACOBS

MILLS & BOON LIMITED
ETON HOUSE   18-24 PARADISE ROAD
RICHMOND   SURREY   TW9 1SR

First published in Great Britain 1991
by Mills & Boon Limited

© Lynn Jacobs 1991

Australian copyright 1991
Philippine copyright 1991
This edition 1991

ISBN 0 263 77164 4

Set in Times Roman 10 on 10½ pt.
01-9107-61851 C

Made and printed in Great Britain

CHAPTER ONE

BOARDING the ferry had been the usual no-holds-barred scrum. Jane had been nearly trampled underfoot by several small, black-clad Greek grandmothers who looked too frail to do anything unaided. She rubbed a bruised rib thoughtfully. She should have remembered that deference and courtesy got you nowhere in these circumstances. Or rather, what they got you was the position of last aboard the boat and a fairly hopeless prospect of finding anywhere with any degree of comfort to pass the rest of the night.

Once she reached the upper deck she was unsurprised to discover the lounge already full and littered with the sprawled, sleeping bodies of other tourists, heads pillowed on rucksacks or on bright hand-woven Greek blankets like the one tucked into her own bag. The thought of a night on deck did not worry her: there was a good chance that she would find a seat inside when passengers departed at Rhodes and, until then, she looked forward to enjoying the soft Aegean night. And to being on her own again. Even the numbers of anonymous bodies scattered around her did not affect that private pleasure. The two weeks' holiday with her friends had been a delight: there had been sun and swimming, long afternoons sprawled lazily in the shade of pine and olive trees, and laughter late into the night over bottles of *retsina* with the sound of Greek music spilling into the darkness as they sat outside the taverna; but Jane had always needed time to herself occasionally. Besides, it had been becoming clear over the last few days that what had begun as an equal, easy relationship between Sheila, Bill and herself was blossoming into something else in which Jane was redundant. She grinned in the darkness. Sheila had hugged her as they said goodbye at the ferry terminal. 'Fancy being a bridesmaid?' she'd whispered.

That would make the third time in a year. Jane wasn't superstitious and was already wondering what to buy as a wedding present. For herself, life had far too much to offer at the moment to make her want to tie herself down to what she tended to think of as marriage, mortgage and motherhood. Not that her own mother was much of an example for her, she decided with an affectionately wry expression on her face.

She settled herself as comfortably as was possible on the narrow wooden slats of the bench seat, tugging her voluminous khaki skirt around her knees. A headscarf was restraining her usually exuberant hair and a man's black shirt would hide any grime she might collect on a journey of over twenty-four hours. She grimaced. It was hardly a flattering outfit but it was certainly functional—and there wasn't anyone around she wanted to impress.

In fact the only people immediately around her seemed to be a small group who, if the off-key singing and raucous laughter were anything to go by, were beyond being impressed by anything. She grimaced as she listened: why was it so often the *English* tourists who made such a spectacle of themselves?

'Let's try the bar!' The suggestion came from a tall blonde girl who wasn't quite steady on her feet.

Yes, do, urged Jane silently, hoping for a quiet night. She was relieved when, after some incoherent discussion, the group moved off, leaving her in possession of the bench. And the sought-for peace.

She wondered idly if she should dig out her notebook and add a few more words to the comments she had already written about travel in Greece, but there wasn't much light to write by and, besides, it was a pleasure just to sit and soak up the atmosphere. The bench might be hard and unyielding, but the scenery made everything worthwhile. Behind the boat the scattered lights of the small town were already receding fast, while above the stars were brightening in the indigo blue of the sky. The thud of the ferry's engines was a dull throb against the rush of water round its bow as it cut through the calm sea. The moon would be up later. What could be more idyllic?

She stretched her feet along the empty bench, glad of this oasis of space among all the general clutter. Something stirred in the deeper shadow cast by the bulwark, just beyond her case. Abruptly the night was no longer a refuge. She peered into the darkness. Yes, there was someone there. A figure, male, she thought, was huddled in the corner. There was nothing to distinguish him from any of the hundred other tourists who thronged the deck—so why the sudden shock of awareness that had jerked her back to reality?

Cautiously, Jane tried to see more, but the light, or its absence, baffled her. He had not moved again after that first brief stirring but somehow his stillness suggested tension, not sleep. Stop it, your imagination's getting out of hand, she told herself, and tried to focus again on the scenery around her. Somehow, it had lost its appeal. This was nonsense. In a boat as crowded as this one, she would be an idiot to expect the seat next to her *not* to be occupied. If she hadn't minded all those sleeping bodies she'd stepped over to find this increasingly hard bench, what on earth was worrying her about this one? She looked again. Not a movement. Resolutely, she closed her eyes. She might as well try to sleep.

It was no good. Sleep wasn't going to come to order. At the far end of the bench the indistinct figure stirred again, and groaned.

'Damn.' The slurred voice was full of exasperation and she opened her eyes to see him fumble for, and drop, a bottle of water. As it lay, emptying itself into one of the salty pools along the deck, he made no effort to reach for it.

Jane's first reaction was to ignore him. If he was drunk, as she suspected, it was his own fault. Then she saw he was simply sitting there, almost defeated, and a reluctant blend of irritation and curiosity drove her into action. She took her own water bottle from her bag.

'I've got plenty of water. Have some of this,' she offered.

He looked up. The deck lighting was fitful and she could not see his features at all, but she thought his hair was fair or light brown. There were shadows on his rather thin face and she suspected he had not shaved recently. Nothing at all to alarm her, she told herself. But something in his sudden stillness made her wonder whether she should have kept quiet. He was more alert than she had thought and she began to revise her initial opinion of his helplessness. He was staring at her and, oddly uncomfortable, she wondered what he was seeing. Whatever it was, he relaxed slightly. At once, that unreasonable sense of danger passed. Her imagination was clearly working overtime again.

He took the bottle she was holding out. 'Thanks.'

At least she had been right in one assumption: he was English. He took the bottle in a hand that was not quite steady and she watched him hold it with a concentration which spoke of a very deliberate control. After several long mouthfuls he sat, breathing deeply and looking at the deck as though to steady himself. She began to wonder if he really was drunk, after all. There was an intentness about his cautious movements that didn't fit with the cheerful group of revellers she had seen earlier and assumed he belonged to.

He seemed to be recovering. He handed back the bottle with another curt word of thanks; then he seemed to forget her, staring out at the cobalt sea as though seeing something there far darker than the swell of the water and the brief flicker of star-shine on the waves. Imagination again. She watched him for a moment longer and then turned away, feeling uncomfortably as though she had intruded on someone's privacy.

That was absurd. The man was a total stranger. Why was she feeling so unreasonably curious about him? Tucking her feet under her, she leaned her head against her bag and shut her eyes again.

The trouble was that the bag was lumpy and the bench already too hard. Minutes later, she opened her eyes. The stranger was standing over her.

She hadn't heard him move and a sudden, irrational fear of robbery, or worse, made her flinch for a moment, wondering if his earlier appearance of weakness had been a ruse.

Eyes, whose colour she couldn't see in the dim light, narrowed at her quick movement. Then the brief, inexplicable moment of tension eased. Something that might even have been intended as a chuckle came from him.

'Relax.' His voice was a mocking drawl. 'I was just going to ask you to keep an eye on my bag for a minute.' It was only half a question.

'Yes, I'll look after it,' she found herself agreeing, puzzled. Was he off to the bar? Perhaps that crowd hadn't had any connection with him—his brooding calm had none of their carefree cheerfulness. She watched idly as he walked away.

Mentally, she shrugged. Minding his bag was not likely to prove particularly taxing. Who on earth did he think was going to steal a very battered old duffel-bag on a ferry that was at least six hours from its next port of call? She moved it so that it was nearer her own bag. It was unexpectedly heavy. Had he left her with a bomb, or was he merely smuggling antiquities? While amused at her own characteristically improbable imaginings, she couldn't help wondering what there was about the stranger that had made her cast him in her mind as some sort of exotic adventurer. Lack of sleep, she told herself, and didn't quite believe it. And the bag *was* oddly heavy.

To herself, at least, she was willing to admit that curiosity was a vice she had not yet managed to overcome. She drew the bag nearer and, unknotting the intricate tangle of frayed cords which held its neck closed, peered inside.

Well, at least there was some reason for his concern. That looked, even to her inexpert eye, like a very expensive and sophisticated camera. She closed and re-knotted the cords. Did offering him water automatically mean she wasn't a camera thief? Or had he been obliquely warning her not to make the attempt? Such reasoning was surely far too devious for a man in his state. Then she remembered his disturbingly quick reactions and surprising alertness, and was less certain.

He was coming back now, still moving with an air of deliberate control. For a moment he was directly under one of the feeble decklights, looking towards her. She got to her feet, fast.

'You're ill!' She took his free arm, supporting him the last few paces to the bench. What she had seen in the set determination of his narrow face had been suffering, not intoxication.

'Observant of you.' He seemed unimpressed by her concern. He put his head in his hands again as he sat down and she saw that his hair was wet. He must have been trying to clear his head under the tap. The surprisingly strong hand that had gripped her shoulder as she helped him had felt hot and dry.

'I thought you were drunk,' she explained.

'I wish I were.' Grim humour touched his voice. 'I don't suppose you...?' he added hopefully.

'Not a drop. Have some more water.' She passed him the bottle. 'So those weren't your friends here earlier on?' she concluded, recalling the drunken tourists.

He frowned. 'Who?' he demanded, looking at her as though suddenly on guard. Then he remembered. 'You mean that lot making all the noise? No,' he confirmed with conviction, wincing as though his headache had suddenly worsened. 'No friends of mine.'

She rummaged in her bulky shoulder-bag. At least there was one practical thing she could do. 'You'd better take these with that water.' She held out the small white pills.

'What are they?' The voice was suspicious and he didn't move.

'Aspirin. Go on: they can't do much harm.'

He shook his head, wincing again, but eventually, when she simply continued to offer the tablets, took them as though it was easier than attempting to argue. The look he gave her held more than a hint of exasperation. He must have seen that she had moved his bag because he lifted it back towards him. Something about the way that she had retied the cords seemed to catch his attention.

He glanced at her. 'Curiosity satisfied?' he asked drily.

She felt the irritating blush that her fair skin made so visible and hoped that the dim light had hidden it. Embarrassment and guilt made her cross. 'Yes,' she snapped. No one in his condition had any right to notice little things like that. She turned her back, emphasising her intention of sleeping.

Minutes dragged past slowly. There was no sound from the man beside her and she wondered if he was still conscious. Probably. Despite the marks burned in his face by fever, she felt uncomfortably aware of his vitality. She began to wish she hadn't interfered. Then she remembered the tranquil night she had been anticipating and grinned to herself: given the chance she knew she always did tend to interfere—it was her besetting sin.

Unconvincing thoughts of waking in the morning to find a corpse beside her began to be displaced by a growing conviction that she was never going to sleep in the first place. Especially if she didn't put on something warm. Despite the earlier heat of the day, the night air was becoming cold as well as clammily damp.

She turned and unzipped her bag. Somewhere in there was a large fisherman's jersey which had survived a trip like this before. Her companion stirred as she moved. She looked at him critically. Ragged jeans and a T-shirt might be normal tourist wear, but they weren't much use to a sick man on a cold night. She dug a bit further in the lumpy bag.

'You'd better put this on,' she told him, resigned.

'What?' He sounded momentarily confused. His voice was not quite steady, as though that self-control which she had sensed earlier was at last beginning to slip under the onslaught of fever.

'It's a blanket. You're cold.' She spoke as patiently as she could. He really was shivering quite hard and she didn't think it was entirely due to the chill of the night. Suddenly, irrationally, it mattered to her that he was so obviously suffering. He hadn't uttered a word of complaint but something was evidently badly wrong, and she wasn't convinced that his distress was entirely physical. She wondered if, like her, he would rather be thought rude than in need. Well, this time he didn't have to *ask* for help. She stood up and draped the blanket around him.

The warmth seemed to penetrate. He held the edges of the rug and looked up at her. 'Are you a nurse or something?' he demanded. His voice was hoarse and tinged with a rather heavy irony.

'No. A teacher.' It wasn't true any more, but it was the simplest answer. She dived into the folds of her own sweater, but not before she heard his groan.

'Saved by a spinster schoolmarm! What a fate!' The weak voice was edged with a humour that Jane didn't much appreciate.

'What makes you think I'm a spinster?' she demanded indignantly, pulling the baggy jumper defensively around her chilled body.

Eyes that seemed temporarily able to focus looked her up and down. Even in the dim light available, she was suddenly uncomfortable under that almost clinical scrutiny.

'Aren't you?' That irritating thread of amusement was still there.

'Yes,' she admitted crossly, tempted to demand the blanket back. Twenty-four was surely a bit young to be written off as a spinster? The word might be technically accurate but his tone of voice had not been flattering. She did, however, have a very fair idea of what she must look like at the moment, so perhaps he could be excused—except that his own appearance didn't give him much right to judge hers. And why on earth was she blushing again?

She turned her back again. There was nothing more of a practical nature she could do for him, and he had effectively crushed any impulse she might have felt to chat, so she might as well ignore him. With any luck he would leave the boat at Rhodes and then she could re-claim her rug and possibly even find a seat inside. He was being very quiet: was he asleep? She had no intention of looking. She lifted her feet back on to the bench, propped herself as comfortably as she could against her bag, and hoped to doze.

Hours passed. The ferry stopped briefly twice, but few people moved and no one seemed inclined to challenge their possession of such spartan accommodation. Even the drunken crowd who had been around earlier must have found somewhere else to pass out. Jane stayed slumped in the kind of numb semi-consciousness that she suspected was not so very different from her neigh-bour's state. The moon had risen, briefly transforming their mundane world, but even its enchantment could not make her wholly forget the hardness of the bench beneath her.

It was just before six in the morning, with daylight beginning to reveal their unlovely immediate sur-roundings as well as the genuine loveliness of the sea beyond, when they at last approached Rhodes.

The magnificent walls and castle glowed, softly mellow in the early morning light, as they passed through the narrow harbour entrance from the open sea to the sheltered port. On the road that ran along the dock, palm trees waved in the breeze; nearby, yachts swung gently at anchor, and the ancient citadel of the crusaders loomed benevolently over all. Jane forgot the discomforts of the night in the magic of the morning.

Around her, the boat was coming to life. There was much rolling up of mats and hoisting of rucksacks and gathering at the head of the stairs, even though it would probably be another twenty minutes before the ship's iron gates clanged open on the dock. The man wrapped in her rug had not moved. She reached out and touched his shoulder.

'What?' He looked up, immediately wide awake. For a moment Jane had the foolish impression that he had been expecting, even fearing, to see someone else. Annoyed at herself, she dismissed the idea. What *was* there about this unkempt stranger that so compelled her interest? She told herself firmly that it was no more than the concern she would have felt for anyone who had needed her aid. Then she sighed: lying to herself never worked.

'Is this where you get off?' she asked prosaically as he began to show signs of impatience.

'That depends where it is,' he said unhelpfully. He didn't seem very interested.

'Rhodes.' Two could be curt.

That got him. He stood up, glancing at her briefly before surveying the grandeur of the harbour. For a moment something softened the severity of his drawn features.

'It certainly is,' he agreed quietly, looking around with interest. The appreciation in his voice thawed Jane towards him—until he spoiled it with his next sentence. 'You can wake me at Crete if you're still on duty.' He lay back and closed his eyes.

His speech, she realised, was educated, even cultured. The manners he was assuming might fit the shabby clothes but they had nothing at all to do with the way he spoke. Was he deliberately trying to put her off? Jane smiled. Any of her friends could have told him that arousing her curiosity was the worst possible way of getting rid of her.

The clatter of anchoring and the noise of the disembarking hordes apparently failed to disturb him. She eyed the equally large crowds waiting to board and knew she had to act at once if she wanted a seat. She picked up her bag. The man was unlikely to make off with her blanket but some irritating thread of concern—or curiosity—made her think that he too would be better off inside. Was he really asleep or had he just switched off? The few words they had so far exchanged made her hesitant to judge only by his appearance of unconsciousness.

If he wants to move, all he has to do is stand up, she told herself. I'll even give him a hand if he asks. It seemed an unlikely possibility. He didn't look as though he was used to asking help from anyone. She wondered briefly why she felt so certain about that, then she dismissed the thought.

She fought her way against the tide of departing passengers and into the emptying lounge. There were only a few sleeping bodies in there now. With cheerful disregard for the people waiting to board, she ensured her comfort for the rest of the journey by spreading her belongings over two seats. This was a great improvement on the open air: the seats were upholstered and would recline like aircraft seats if she wanted, and it even looked as though the snack bar at the far end of the lounge was about to resume business.

She had firmly intended to sit down and relax every stiff and cramped joint as soon as she could but, somehow, the memory of her companion would not let her. Calling herself all sorts of fool, she spread her luggage far enough to encompass another seat, and went back outside.

Unsurprisingly, he was still there. It didn't look as though he'd moved. She had no idea what his name was, she realised, and somehow 'Hey, mister...' didn't sound right, so she touched his arm. He lifted his head and sighed.

'Hello again. Is this Crete?' Sarcasm, not interest, marked his voice. He showed no surprise at all at seeing her and Jane was convinced he hadn't been asleep.

'No. It's still Rhodes—as you can see—and I've found you a seat inside,' she told him.

'I'm very comfortable here,' he said, his voice dismissive. She ignored the implied rejection.

'No, you're not. No one could be. Come on, you'll be better off inside.'

He just looked at her. She supposed she had used the tone of voice she might have chosen for a junior pupil, but he had asked for it. It was disconcerting, however, to discover just how quelling his eyes could be. But she could be stubborn, too. And cunning. Before he could anticipate her actions, she picked up his precious duffel bag and walked off with it.

She had read him accurately. Two minutes later he was sitting beside her in the lounge, glaring.

'Who on earth do you think you are? Goody-Two-Shoes?' he demanded, his exasperation clear.

'Something like that,' she admitted, 'but you can call me Jane.'

He didn't relax, and she was fairly certain he was still annoyed at her high-handed approach, but something that just might have been a flicker of amusement showed in his eyes. They were a cool, clear grey, she was interested to notice. For some reason she had assumed they would be blue. His hair was a light brown, his thin face, with its marked cheekbones, was tanned and, although at the moment it was compressed in a line of irritation, she suspected his mouth might normally be expressively mobile.

'Don't think I'm going to ask you to call me Tarzan,' he warned, evidently aware of her scrutiny.

She looked him over. Revenge could be sweet and she hadn't forgiven that earlier crack about spinster school-marms. For once she was not going to look away and blush—there was a challenge in his hostility that she couldn't quite resist.

'I wouldn't dream of it,' she told him sweetly. 'You haven't the physique.'

She was lying. He was no over-developed weight-lifter, but the T-shirt and tight-fitting jeans revealed a body that was athletically lean and had some impressive muscles. As he had walked, or perhaps the right word was *stalked*, across the lounge towards her she hadn't missed the easy grace with which he had moved, despite his illness. Perhaps if she had seen that aspect of him earlier she would have been less ready to provoke him. Even now, she was beginning to wonder just how foolish she had been, but it wasn't in her nature to retreat. Besides, though she had an odd feeling that he could be dangerous, she had an equally irrational conviction that—despite his temper—she was not at risk. And she was still curious.

'Well? What *do* I call you?' she asked when her retort produced nothing more than a sardonic chuckle and a slight relaxation of the tight lips.

'John Smith?' he suggested amiably. Clearly he had no intention of giving anything away.

She raised what she hoped was a disbelieving eyebrow at the obvious lie. 'All right, "John Smith",' she said. 'Do you want some bread and coffee?'

'Is there no end to your benevolence?' he sighed. He sounded as though he wished there were, but then he seemed to have second thoughts. 'Coffee...?' he wondered with a little more interest.

She passed him her penknife and a slightly stale loaf. 'Hack a couple of hunks off that. I'll get the coffee before the next queue starts up. Greek or Nes?' She named the abbreviation that covered every sort of badly made instant coffee throughout Greece.

He shuddered. 'You need to ask?'

Jane grinned, suddenly liking him. 'Two Greek coffees coming up.'

She was back in five minutes with a tray holding two glasses of iced water and two tiny cups of strong black coffee. 'Breakfast,' she told him, 'is served.'

He took the tray from her and balanced it between them on her bag. His, she noticed, was tucked firmly beneath his seat. He seemed to be coming back to life.

'You're getting better,' she said, observing this.

'I'm beginning to believe I might live,' he agreed. He was looking at her curiously and she was uncomfortably aware of her rather tatty headscarf and bulky clothes. 'Do you make a habit of this?' he said, just as she was starting to wonder whether she ought to apologise for her appearance.

'Of what?' For a moment she was puzzled.

'Impounding stray dogs. Bullying defenceless invalids back to health. Things like that,' he explained with a vague gesture. His hands were thin and long-fingered, but there was nothing weak about them. Jane remembered the strength of his grasp on her shoulder earlier that night.

'No.' She chewed a chunk of dry bread, trying to remember her original impulse which was now rather confused by her more personal interest in the man who called himself 'John Smith'. 'It's just that you were in the only part of the boat that seemed to have any space left for me to sit down. I thought you might be drunk and didn't want any trouble,' she added with deliberately provocative honesty.

'Pure self-interest, in fact?' He sounded as though he approved. And she had been right about that mouth: its softened lines revealed unoffended amusement at her candour.

'As pure as it comes,' she agreed cheerfully. At least he was looking at her now as though she was a person and not merely an irritation. Fleetingly, she was conscious of an unexpectedly powerful wish that her ferry clothes weren't *quite* so unrevealingly dowdy.

'And just now...?' He indicated their present surroundings, reminding her that she had more or less forced him inside.

She shrugged. She had no intention of analysing the mixture of emotions that might have aroused her compulsive concern for his well-being. 'I didn't want you going off with my blanket,' she told him. Before he could ask the obvious next question, she added, 'And you only got the blanket in the first place because I didn't want to find myself sharing the bench with a corpse. Satisfied?'

'Entirely.' His voice was bland as he went on, 'You could just have pushed my body overboard. Think of all the extra space you'd have gained.'

'I'm beginning to wish I had thought of it,' she lied. She wasn't used to being on the wrong end of verbal sparring, or to feeling defensive about what had, after all, been a gesture of kindness on her part. She was going to have to assert her indifference. 'I intend to get some sleep now that it's possible. If you get off at Crete, don't wake me: I'm going on to Athens.' She curled more comfortably on the padded seat, glad that she was short enough to do so, and tried to ignore her neighbour.

Rather to her surprise, she slept deeply for over three hours. When she woke it was to full daylight and to find 'John Smith' watching her with a smile that she deeply mistrusted on his thin face. His duffel bag was in his hands and, as he saw her eyes open, he swiftly reknotted the cords and bent to replace it beneath his seat.

'What have you been up to?' she demanded suspiciously.

He spread his hands in a wholly unconvincing gesture of innocence. 'Nothing. Would I?' he challenged.

Jane looked down at her crumpled self. Even without the sweater she had to admit that she still looked far from her best. The headscarf had slipped low on her forehead and she pushed it back. 'Probably not at the moment,' she acknowledged ruefully, trying to suppress a moment's foolish regret at her evident lack of appeal. That was nonsense: he looked far worse than she did. Then she was less sure.

He definitely seemed to be regaining his health. The pallor that had edged his mouth and the shadows under his eyes had receded. Although he still looked as though he hadn't shaved or slept for several days, there was something almost rakishly compelling about him this morning. She began to feel slightly uneasy; if she had caught that unsettlingly challenging glint in his eyes when she had first encountered him, she might not have been quite so quick to interfere.

Then he gave a short splutter of laughter, probably at her disgruntled expression, she thought sourly, and abruptly the dangerous rake was possessed of an equally—if not more—dangerous charm. It was far too easy to like someone who could laugh at himself.

'Where did you get on board?' she asked. If he was going to be human, she might even manage to satisfy her curiosity.

'Kos.' The one-word answer was not encouraging.

'Did you like it?' she persevered, wondering why she was bothering.

He sighed. 'I don't know. I was only there for a day, then I caught the first ferry out. It seemed like a good place to be ill in peace,' he added pointedly.

'We all make mistakes. I was staying on Nissiros,' she told him since he clearly wasn't going to ask.

'Alone?' It sounded as though he could see why.

'Travelling alone. I met up with two other friends there. But they're staying for another couple of weeks.

I wanted a couple of days in Athens before flying back to England. They,' she added with a rueful smile, 'aren't much interested in any sights at the moment except each other.'

He glanced down at her without much sympathy. 'In the way, were you?'

The comment was barbed, but it didn't hurt. Neither Bill nor Sheila had made her feel unwanted and romance had been the last thing on their minds when they had decided, months ago, to travel together. On the whole, Jane felt rather pleased with the outcome of two weeks in the sun for her friends.

'Not really,' she dismissed the remark, 'but I'm looking forward to Athens. As a *teacher*,' she stressed the word, enjoying his wince, privately also enjoying the fact that she never intended to teach again, 'I get decent length holidays and I like to make the most of them. Fascinating, isn't it?' she added, reading his expression without any difficulty.

'Riveting. Do you mind if I spare you my life story? I'm not into girlish confidences.' Jane believed him. He didn't look as though he ever let anyone behind that offhand façade. The mixture of flippancy and self-control was intriguing—but she had no intention of betraying her interest.

'That's all right. If it's anything like as convincing as your name, I wouldn't believe it anyway,' she told him cheerfully. He looked blank for a moment. 'You told me your name was John Smith,' she reminded him with satisfaction. 'There's no point in assuming an alias if even you can't remember it.'

'Thank you. I'll write it down somewhere,' he said gravely, his lips twitching. But he showed no sign of telling her what his real name might be.

Exchanging edged comments with an anonymous stranger, particularly this one, was certainly more entertaining than most ways Jane had yet found of killing time on a long journey. Although he dozed on and off for most of the day, he wasn't unwilling to talk, or at least to let her talk, when he was awake. She told him a little about the school she had worked at and outlined her plans for the rest of the holiday; but she learned nothing at all about him, except that he intended to fly directly back to England from Crete.

Eventually, with the evening drawing on, the boat's anchor clattered down in the small Cretan harbour of Sitia. 'John Smith' stood up and stretched. Jane was oddly disappointed as she realised that their curious companionship was at an end.

'You're leaving here? Wouldn't Agios Nikolaos be easier for you?' She named the other Cretan port the ferry called at, knowing it didn't stop at the main town of Heraklion.

'Sitia will do fine,' he said, his voice neutral.

She got to her feet uncertainly. It had been a long day but this parting seemed to be happening unexpectedly quickly. She saw him reach under the seat for his bag.

'At least your precious luggage is safe,' she said, surprised by the faint edge to her voice.

An odd smile touched his mouth. 'I certainly hope so. I've gone to enough trouble carting it around.'

The bag wasn't that heavy. 'Are you going to be all right?' Curiosity mingled with her concern.

'Are you going to abandon your tour of Athens in favour of my fevered brow if I say no? If I were you, I'd wait to be asked,' he finished nastily, and she flushed.

'Oh, go to hell,' she told him, exasperation easily conquering sympathy.

An odd look crossed his face. 'I probably will,' he told her and then, almost unwillingly she thought, added, 'But first——'

Before she could recognise his intention, he had pulled her roughly towards him and kissed her. Hard. It certainly wasn't a thank-you for her help. Stubble grazed her cheek and there was at least as much insult as desire in the kiss and the embrace which accompanied it. She didn't even have time to respond, never mind slap his face or stamp on his foot, before he let her go, an unrepentant grin on his thin face and a speculative look in the cool grey eyes.

'Don't expect an apology,' he told her before she could speak. 'You've been asking for trouble since we met. I must say, though,' he went on thoughtfully, his voice touched with laughter and some other, less obvious, reaction, 'there's more, or perhaps it's less, to you than meets the eye under those jumble sale cast-offs you're wearing. Perhaps I should have investigated earlier.'

She didn't *think* he was serious. But she didn't quite know how to take the glint in those clear eyes. 'The other passengers are leaving,' she pointed out as frostily as she could despite a suddenly, and infuriatingly, quickened pulse. He didn't look away and she found her own eyes held by his and felt the colour mount in her face.

'So they are. I wonder...' But she was not to know what he wondered because he shrugged and said only, 'It was probably a lousy idea any. Goodbye, Florence Nightingale.'

His voice softened unexpectedly on the last words, but somehow there wasn't anything she could say. He looked at her for a moment longer as though still debating something with himself, and then he turned abruptly, and walked away.

'Goodbye, "John Smith",' Jane murmured to herself, feeling oddly forlorn. On impulse she followed him out on to the deck. Minutes later she looked down on the dock and he was only a brown-blond head among the crowd, barely distinguishable from a hundred others. In fact, it was surprising that she was able to pick him out so easily.

CHAPTER TWO

JANE had four days in Athens before her flight home and no wish to waste any of them. She planned to wander round the shops and museums and parks, buy a few last-minute presents for friends and generally enjoy the contrasts between city life and lotus-eating on the island— not to mention the rigours of the ferry. It was irritating to discover just how often during the next few days that memories of that ferry journey and, inevitably, of 'John Smith' came back into her mind, even when she should have been absorbed by the magnificence of some of the exhibits in the Archaeological Museum.

Unsatisfied curiosity, that was all it was, she told herself daily whenever she recalled the details of their short acquaintance. His vivid face, with its sudden laughter and guarded stillnesses, was clear in her memory and she still didn't know whether she liked or resented his offhand flippancy and apparent cynicism. Perhaps her interest was just piqued vanity: he'd made it clear that she was far from being the most appealing woman he'd met. Yes, she had looked a wreck—and, even at her best, she didn't rate her looks very highly—but he'd hardly been in a position to complain. And she could hardly call that kiss a complaint, her other self reminded her. As if she had been able to forget her uncomfortably intense reaction to something that had surely been nothing more than his way of getting the last word.

Jane shook her head, annoyed at the way that particular memory tended to steal up on her. She was surprised it was still so clear. One day it would surely make one of those entertaining holiday anecdotes for her friends back in England. It was absurd to feel reluctant to tell anyone about her encounter with a rude and dishevelled stranger whose name she didn't know—and probably never would. They weren't, after all, likely to meet again.

She should have known better. If she had learned anything about 'John Smith' on that journey, it was that he was unpredictable. When she opened the door to her hotel room at mid-morning on her third day in Athens, a curious sense of inevitability touched a deep chord somewhere in her beneath the immediate shock of recognition.

'Hello,' she heard herself saying blankly. She wasn't quite sure how she had recognised him so immediately: the unkempt stranger of her memory had disappeared. The man regarding her from the doorway was relaxed and confident and immaculately dressed. And amused. That familiar, barely hidden laughter brought her to her senses. 'Fancy seeing you here,' she commented tartly, hoping he had not noticed the jolt to her senses that the sight of him had caused.

'Yes, it is a small world,' he agreed drily, matching her cliché with his own in a way that made her smile. Imperceptibly, she relaxed.

'I gather you didn't linger on Crete?' She *wasn't* going to ask him how he had found her. Or why.

'I only ever intended to stay long enough to pick up some things,' he told her—as usual, explaining nothing, she realised, but couldn't resist chuckling as he added wickedly, 'I hadn't got a *thing* to wear.'

'You've clearly been shopping,' she said more cheerfully, taking in the fashionable clothes. 'What brings you to the Hotel Amazon?' Well, it wasn't really a direct question about how he had found her, she told herself defensively.

He grinned, but didn't explain. 'I owed you a meal,' he said instead, 'and I always pay my debts. Besides, I couldn't get a direct flight to London from Crete—they were all full of schoolchildren and teachers,' he added with mocking emphasis.

She wasn't listening. 'A meal?' For a moment she was bewildered.

'Breakfast.' He reminded her of the coffee and stale bread they had shared. 'But I'm offering lunch in return. What do you think?'

'What I think——' she began impulsively, then checked herself. This might be her only chance to satisfy her curiosity. She glanced down at her casual cotton trousers and back at his more elegant attire. 'Half an hour?' she suggested.

'I'll meet you in the lobby,' he agreed, smiling as he turned away. As she closed the door behind him she realised he'd smiled more in the last five minutes than in the whole twenty-four hours of their ferry journey. And the smile was not without its effect.

Thoughtfully, she leaned her back against the door, and took a deep breath. He might be more cheerful, in fact he had seemed positively light-hearted, but that didn't necessarily make him safe company. She prided herself on her honesty and her reaction to his reappearance in her life was more extreme than their brief encounter justified. Until she had opened the door to him she hadn't even realised that she had been finding Athens, with all its variety and vibrant energy, almost dull. Then she had felt herself come to life under the lazy amusement of his gaze. Yes, he was definitely *not* safe. If she had any of the common sense people kept congratulating her on she would stay up here and let him wait in the lobby till he took the hint and shrugged his elegantly clad shoulders and walked out of her life. She glimpsed her own wry smile in the wardrobe mirror as she reached in to take out her only really smart dress. Common sense didn't stand a chance.

She just had time for a shower. She washed quickly and brushed out her short blonde curls. With her clear brown eyes her hair colouring sometimes surprised people, but the unusual combination gave her looks a distinctive appeal which she suspected they would not otherwise possess. She had neat, regular features and an engaging smile, but she did not fool herself that she was a raving beauty. She was genuinely unaware of the appeal that her vitality and quick humour lent to her looks, or of the natural grace which marked her movements. She reached for the dress, glad that it was uncreased, reminding herself that raving beauties tended to be four or five inches taller than her, and probably a pound or two lighter. No one would call her plump, but her very feminine curves weren't those of a fashionable model.

She surveyed her reflection critically. The dress suited her. Its dropped waist and blouson top flattered her figure and the shades of green went well with her colouring, showing off her clear skin and golden tan. A good thing: she didn't have much choice. She remembered how the transformed 'John Smith' had looked: he had been wearing white cotton trousers and a short-sleeved blue shirt. An expensive-looking linen jacket had been held casually over his shoulder by one thumb hooked in its neckline. He had borne, she thought as she applied a light lip gloss and fastened a string of fake pearls round her neck, little resemblance to the feverish stranger on the boat. For a start, she hadn't consciously thought of 'John Smith' as good-looking. Compelling, yes; good-looking, no. This man, with his brown-blond hair and steel-grey eyes, certainly was. In the few days since she had last seen him the gaunt thinness and marks of illness in his face had been transformed into a fine-drawn elegance that she sensed would defy age. At present she guessed he might be a little under thirty. Had she seen him like that, instead of huddled on a bench in the gloom, when they had first met, she would never have approached him. She sent her reflection an un-repentant, and very private grin; she might well have wanted to. She turned towards the door. At least she no longer looked like someone's poor relation, and he would see that 'jumble sale cast-offs' were not her only clothes.

He was waiting, with no sign of impatience, when she emerged from the lift. Grey eyes looked her over.

'That,' he said at last, 'is a considerable improvement on the ferry.'

Her colour heightened, she returned the glance. 'I could say the same of you. What's more, at least I had these clothes with me all along. Yours weren't in that bag,' she challenged. There hadn't been room for anything except the camera.

'You should know,' he said pleasantly. 'You looked.' As a comment, it had the merit of silencing her. 'Shall we go?' he asked, and took a pair of mirrored sunglasses from his jacket pocket.

Jane hated the things. It was frustrating to talk to someone when all you could read in their eyes was your own expression. She suspected, from the slight smile touching his long mouth, that he guessed exactly how she felt.

'Where are we going?' she asked as they crossed Syntagma Square.

'What had you planned?'

She thought for a moment. 'I'd probably have had an ice-cream here and dabbled my feet in the fountain,' she admitted, pointing to the water tumbling into the shallow circular basin.

'What about something more adventurous? The choice is yours.' His look was a challenge.

Did he expect her to pick a taverna in a corner of the Plaka, or the high-priced subdued luxury of the Hotel Grande Bretagne? she wondered. She could eat in the Plaka any time, and the sun was too bright and the day suddenly too cheerful to waste in the shadows of an air-conditioned dining-room. Besides, it was early yet. She looked up at him; he was watching her with an expression of resignation veiling the lurking humour in his face.

'Well?' He must have read her decision in her eyes.

'I've only been up Lykavettos once before,' she told him. 'And I've *never* eaten at the restaurant up there.'

The tall hill which dominated northern Athens, looking down even on the Acropolis, had both breathtaking views and an attractive restaurant at its summit. Jane's funds, however, had previously run to nothing more extravagant than an ice-cream from the stall that served all the hot and weary tourists who emerged on to the hilltop.

'Nor have I,' he surprised her. 'Do you insist on a taxi, or are you feeling fit?'

'A taxi?' It hadn't occurred to her. 'The walk's half the fun. Let's go.' He stayed still. 'What are we waiting for?'

'The lights,' he said drily. 'Try crossing the road against them and not all your nursing skills would do either of us any good.'

Observing the roar and snarl of the traffic, she had to admit that he was right. At last it paused, held at bay by a red light, and they crossed the road.

It didn't take many minutes to leave behind the major roads and their noise and fumes and to enter the maze of small streets, often linked by tree-lined squares, which lay on their uphill route. Neither hurried. This was a part of the city not many tourists visited, where the shops were mostly small and exclusive and the balconies of the apartments above their heads spilled vines and ivy and gaudy bougainvillaea to cloak the whitewashed concrete, and even the cats looked plump and well-fed.

In Jane's experience, men were useless at window-shopping. She should have known 'John Smith' would prove an exception. He seemed to take as much delight as she did in examining the lovely, intricate modern jewellery in one shop window, or speculating about the age and origins of the icons in another. She was surprised by how much he knew about art. Then he grabbed her hand, halting her, chuckling, in front of a display which seemed to contain every possible extravagance and extreme of bad modern fashion. Absently, because most of her feelings were focused on the odd rush of sensation that the sudden clasp on her fingers had produced, Jane noticed that those prices which were visible seemed to include an improbable number of noughts.

'Right,' he told her. 'You simply have to have something—what do you choose?'

Her gaze travelled slowly from the purple fox-stole in which the depressed-looking creature's eyes had been replaced by glittering fake diamonds—at least she assumed they were fakes—to the brief and figure-hugging black chiffon dress only preserved from indecency by strategic designs in yet more glitter. She looked back to her companion, who was examining the clothes with apparent admiration. He had removed the offending glasses in the shady street and she didn't miss the glint of challenge in the sidelong glance he gave her. She never could resist a dare.

'It's just got to be that one,' she decided, pointing.

He looked from her to the satin leopard-skin body suit, and back again. 'The imagination reels,' he murmured.

It was infuriating to find that the bland look really had seemed to reclothe her in something infinitely more revealing than her own dress, and that her body had tightened unfamiliarly in response to a moment's fire in those usually cool grey eyes. She looked away, and was glad to see another shop where she could continue the game and ignore that sudden moment of awareness and the warmth in her cheeks. She gestured with her free hand.

'Your turn. *You* have to choose a souvenir.' She told herself that the breathy catch in her voice was entirely the fault of the steep hill they were climbing.

He was apparently torn between a glossy white marble reproduction of the Acropolis, complete with internal lighting, and an almost life-size Aphrodite stepping off her scallop shell and upholding a standard lamp in the hand that wasn't clutching her pastel pink draperies.

'She'd look better in leopard-skin,' he decided eventually. And they walked on, looking at other shops which held books and glass and rugs that they really could imagine wanting. But he didn't release her hand and she didn't try to tug her fingers free from his. He might consider it, if he thought about it at all, just a friendly gesture, but Jane was beginning to feel as though it were a connection to some new and vibrant form of energy which made the sky a brighter blue and every sound and scent and sight unexpectedly fresh and new. It might be dangerous to tap such energy, but here, for a few hours, out in the open where nothing else could happen, she was going to enjoy it.

The steep streets gave way to flights of steps between houses and apartments where terracotta pots of brilliant geraniums and brightly painted tubs of basil added colour and scent to the day. The hill of Lykavettos loomed above them and Jane began to feel the ache of the climb in her legs. She turned where the steps flattened out momentarily to survey the city spreading below them. And to catch her breath. At least no one would notice now if she blushed: she was far too hot from her exertions. Beside her, her companion seemed wholly unaffected by the climb. He was breathing as easily as though they were taking a casual stroll, and he had replaced those wretched sunglasses as they emerged into the sunlight, so his face was unrevealing.

'Ready to go on?' he wondered after a minute or two.

Defiantly, she took her hand from his. 'If you are,' she snapped and turned towards the next flight of steps. She wasn't going to stop again if it killed her. Behind her she thought she heard the ghost of a chuckle, but she didn't look.

It didn't kill her. The two weeks of swimming and walking on the island had made her fairly fit, but she was glad to reach the doors to the short funicular railway which would take them up the last few yards.

He bought their tickets and they travelled almost in silence up the steepest part of the ascent. They were alone in the little cabin and, for the first time since they had set out, Jane began to feel oddly awkward in his company. As they emerged from the dark tunnel into the windswept brightness of the hilltop she walked quickly out and up on to the parapet. He was not far behind; she could feel his eyes on her and all the exhilaration of earlier was replaced by something far less comfortable. She knew nothing at all about him, she thought with sudden clarity. Was he really interested in her? Or in repaying an imaginary debt as he had claimed? Both seemed improbable. He certainly hadn't shown much sense of gratitude on the ferry, and she was hardly the type to persuade exotic-looking strangers to search half a city for her. And, anyway, just how *had* he found her?

She stared at the city spread out below her, dominated by the dramatic architecture of the Parthenon, the busy streets disappearing into the haze over Piraeus and the docks. She didn't see a thing. 'John Smith' stepped up to join her.

'Fabulous, isn't it?' he said quietly.

'Yes.' She'd no idea what he'd asked. 'How did you know where I was staying?' she demanded abruptly, furious with herself for asking.

He chuckled, interpreting her anger without apparent difficulty. 'I read luggage labels,' he told her. 'I remember thinking at the time that the Hotel Amazon was a singularly appropriate place for you to be staying.'

'You've been to a lot of trouble for a total stranger,' she said slowly. She had thought on the ferry that he was more alert than a person in his condition had any right to be. This confirmed it. Be careful, she warned herself again, you could be getting out of your league.

He shrugged at her comment, lazy grey eyes dismissing the panoramic view to focus for a moment on her and she wondered just how easily he read her. All he said was, 'I told you, I like to pay my debts.'

It was just a casual remark, but she had the odd feeling that it was also something more significant than that to him. He didn't seem inclined to explain any further, though.

'Lunch?' he suggested. 'The view's almost as good from the restaurant and we could both do with a cold drink.'

At least he had the grace to imply that the climb had been demanding for both of them. She didn't believe for a moment that he'd felt much strain, but it was a pleasant change for him to be behaving like a gentleman. It was probably unreasonable that his access of good behaviour should bring out that streak of stubbornness in her. She didn't move away from the railing and he turned back with a quizzical frown.

'Lunch?' he repeated.

'On one condition,' she said firmly.

It was surprising how quickly wariness could replace amusement in a face with only a fractional change of expression. Relaxed ease had become caution. 'Which is?' His voice was as light as ever, his tone distinctly cool.

'I can't keep calling you "John Smith",' she explained. 'It doesn't suit you.'

Why should *that* make him relax? Jane wondered what he had expected her to ask.

'That's probably because it's not my name,' he agreed amicably.

'I'd gathered that,' she said carefully, determined not to be exasperated by him. Or to give up. 'So what *are* you called?'

'A variety of things, few of them flattering.' She straightened. Some lunches weren't worth bothering with. He saw her intention and surprised her. 'My name's Craig,' he said quietly. She waited. Somehow it was important that he told her at least this much about himself. 'Craig Stanton. That's more than you told me of yours,' he pointed out. His tone was flippant again but, somehow, their tenuous relationship had another strand woven into it. She felt her own expression relax into a smile.

'It's Jane Simpson. But you already know that because you read luggage labels,' she reminded him. He had been watching her closely but now he seemed at ease again. Had it really been that hard to tell her his name? She felt much better now that she had one that fitted him. It was almost familiar, but that was probably because anything would have sounded right after 'John Smith'. 'Let's have lunch,' she decided, offering her arm in a friendly fashion.

He was looking at her as though unsure whether to laugh or to wring her neck. Good. It was nice to think that, just occasionally, she could bewilder him. He was obviously far too used to being in control of the situation. He took her offered arm and they walked down the steps into the restaurant. When she glanced up at him the grey eyes were warm with laughter and he chuckled as he escorted her to a table.

They ate crisply fried *calamares* and tiny, succulent pieces of lamb on wooden skewers, with a fresh tomato salad and a light Greek wine which seemed to contain the sun's gold. The tension that had hummed between them since they met seemed to have eased. It was still there, in the background, Jane knew, giving spice to the moment and that edge of risk to every exchange, but over the meal they began to talk less like fencers assessing each other's skills and more like people who just might be interested in each other. Since she didn't want to talk about her future plans, she found herself describing the past, including her family, more fully than she was usually willing to.

'My father died last year,' she told him in answer to a question, her voice slightly husky with the memory of grief.

'I'm sorry. And your mother? Do you live with her?' His voice was uncharacteristically gentle.

She laughed aloud at the thought of herself and her mother ever being able to cope with living together. 'Heavens, no. She left Dad when I was ten—not that I ever blamed her; I loved them both dearly but even I could see that they were hopelessly mismatched. She went off to "find herself",' she added, unable to stop herself smiling, although, as a teenager, some of her mother's more extravagant ventures had appalled and embarrassed her. 'What she actually found, after a try at a hippy commune and one more false start in the marriage stakes...' which had helped convince Jane that marriage had far too high a risk factor '...was a very large, very rich Texan called Ben who adores her and is delighted to indulge her frequent impulses to dash off to the back of beyond. I've even got a half-brother,' she finished.

'Do you see them often?' Craig was watching her as though fascinated, toying absently with his glass as he watched the animated play of emotions on her face.

She shook her head. 'Very seldom. Mother and I have a sort of long-distance affectionate relationship. When I decided to teach she decided I was being boringly conventional and really ought to go off in search of Adventure. Or Texans,' she added thoughtfully.

'And will you?' he wondered.

Jane grimaced. 'I doubt it. Mother was probably right about me.' She might have given up teaching, she might even get vague family support for her next move, but she didn't feel like revealing her insubstantial plans to Craig's scorn. She was startled by his sudden laugh. 'What's wrong?'

'I don't think many people would consider someone who goes round picking up invalids on Greek ferries and bullying them back to life as either boring or conventional,' he explained.

'I hate incompetence.' It was a sort of explanation, at least of her first impulse.

'And I was being incompetent?' He raised an eyebrow. It was hard to reconcile his current sleek image with that unshaven figure who had slumped on the bench beside her.

'Thoroughly. I thought you'd given up.' Far safer to confirm her image as a schoolmarm than to try to describe that elusive compulsion which had drawn her to him despite the unpromising surroundings and his total lack of encouragement.

A wry expression crossed his face and his smile held little humour. He ran one thin hand through the brown-blond hair as though disturbed by an unpleasant memory. 'In some ways, I think I had,' he admitted. 'It wasn't an enjoyable twenty-four hours.'

Jane had an impulse to smooth back the hair he had tousled, but prudently restrained herself. He seemed preoccupied, as though recalling something far worse than illness.

'It can't have been,' she agreed, her voice neutral.

He looked down at his empty glass. 'No,' he said and put the glass firmly aside as though marking the end of the subject. Fine. If he didn't want to satisfy her interest in that, he could talk to her about something else.

'So what do you do for a living?' she wondered aloud. Perhaps he didn't do anything. His clothes certainly said money, his easy assurance and educated voice suggested a comfortable background. But no, she didn't see Craig Stanton as a playboy, somehow, even if that was his image today.

'A little bit of this and that.' The casual tone was another closed door.

'And a bit of photography?' she suggested.

'Some,' he agreed. 'Is there anything else you need to know?' The repressive chill in his voice was a marked contrast with his earlier light-heartedness, and Jane was suddenly angry.

'Nothing at all. It's just that I used to think that conversation was a two-way process, that's all. You know the sort of thing: I tell you something and you offer some comment in return. You've found out more than you ever probably wanted to know about my family and I've just about managed to extract your name from you with the aid of a rack and thumbscrews. Great. Thanks for lunch; I'll find my own way back.' As she stood up her chair made an ugly screeching sound against the marble tiles.

She brushed past an agitated-looking waiter on her way out. He was probably worrying about his bill. He needn't: she was sure Craig would observe all the decencies before making any effort at all to follow her. She had plenty of time to get to the little railway before he even made a token gesture of pursuit. Which didn't explain at all why she was standing looking out over the hills beyond Athens with distinctly blurred vision and the feeling that she'd just made a total fool of herself and ruined a perfectly good day out.

'I'm a rich little orphan,' said an unconvincingly meek voice beside her.

She sniffed and did not look at him, resolutely trying to ignore the sudden bubble of internal relief which seemed determined to break out. 'I'm not surprised,' she told him sourly.

He laughed, the moment of suspicion and bad temper clearly gone. 'You think I drove them to an early grave?'

She turned her back on the view to look up at him, but he was against the sun and she couldn't see his expression. Besides, he was sure to despise the quick twist of sympathy that tugged at her in spite of his easy words. 'Either that, or they took one look and abandoned you on the nearest doorstep.' She kept the acid note in her voice.

His answering smile had an ironic twist. 'Not quite. Dad was a much-travelled diplomat. In my "best interests"...' she could feel the careful quotation marks around the remembered words '...they left me to various schools and relatives while they jaunted off around the world. They were killed in a plane crash ten years ago,' he added in a tone which didn't invite comment.

And you don't trust anyone or need anyone in your life to complicate it; Jane heard the warning that he probably didn't even realise he had given. She might have come from a broken home, and she might live alone, but she had never really been lonely and that glimpse into the arctic chill of a child's loneliness both frightened and enraged her. She wanted to tell his parents exactly what she thought of them. But there wasn't much she could safely say to Craig without provoking his derision.

He reached out to touch the curls which the wind was ruffling. 'Perhaps you should have brought a scarf,' he said lightly, and suddenly everything was all right again.

'I only have one scarf,' she told him gravely, and saw his lips twitch at the memory of the ferry.

'It was interesting to discover what you actually looked like without your travelling disguise,' he admitted.

'Jumble sale cast-offs,' she reminded him.

'Precisely. I had a bet with myself that you were a blonde, by the way, despite the golden eyes.' She glanced sharply at him, but his voice was lightly teasing. It was absurd that a single word should momentarily make her heart race. And brown eyes were still brown, after all. 'It wasn't easy to tell in the circumstances,' he admitted. Since the scarf had been designed to protect as much of her hair as possible, she was unsurprised. 'Is it natural?' he asked mildly.

She was beginning to recognise deliberate provocation when she heard it and she managed not to react. 'Absolutely,' she told him, surveying the sun-blond streaks in his light brown hair. 'Is yours?'

She could get to like that sudden, carefree laugh, she thought as he lifted both hands in a gesture of mock-surrender. 'Every streak guaranteed entirely sun-bleached,' he told her in exaggerated parody of an advertiser's smooth-toned assurances. 'One good English winter and it'll be back to normal,' he added in cheerful tones. He wasn't conceited, she realised suddenly. He knew the effect he had on people and he probably used it to get what he wanted when it suited him, but he didn't really care about it at all. One more assumption—that good-looking men were always vain—hit the dust.

By unspoken mutual agreement they moved towards the entrance to the railway. At the bottom, Craig glanced at his watch.

'Let's take a taxi back,' he suggested. 'I'm afraid I've a business appointment later on this afternoon.'

'That's all right,' Jane agreed quickly. She tried to ignore an irrational surge of disappointment. The invitation had only been for lunch, after all, and he'd already told her it was just the repayment of a debt.

'It's a pain,' he said bluntly and her spirits rose. 'We'll have supper together, though, if you like—and don't mind eating late.'

'Does anyone in Athens eat early?' she wondered aloud, remembering once trying to get a meal at seven in the evening.

He grinned. 'Point taken. There's a place in the Plaka you might like,' he suggested. 'It's fairly basic but the food's good and it has a roof-top terrace that's almost nestling against the side of the Acropolis.'

She couldn't help laughing. 'It sounds like the one I found last night—I was planning to go back there anyway. I'll meet you there at nine, if you like.'

'Good. I'm sure I'll be clear by then.'

It was an odd business appointment that would take so long, but she had learned at lunch that he had no intention of discussing his work, whatever it was, with her. Half seriously she wondered for a moment if he was a smuggler or something. If so, she definitely didn't want to know about it until long after today was all over.

Just then the taxi arrived and they were back in central Athens in ten minutes in contrast with the hour they had spent in walking and loitering on their way up.

He started to walk with her across Syntagma Square. 'You don't have to see me back to the hotel,' she protested. 'Don't forget your appointment.'

'I've a couple of hours till then,' he told her. So why had they rushed back? 'But I wanted to take a photo of you and I've left my cameras in the hotel.'

She flushed with absurd pleasure. 'A picture of me? What on earth for?'

He stopped, facing her, and tilted her chin up with one finger so that she was staring straight into his face. And into her own reflection in those wretched glasses. 'Souvenirs, perhaps?' he offered. 'You shouldn't underestimate yourself.'

She didn't. She prided herself on knowing exactly what she was like, and it still didn't make sense. Not that she felt at all inclined to argue, not with his hand still lingering beside her throat and a softer smile than she had seen before touching the corners of his mobile mouth. 'It's your film,' she managed to say with an air of carelessness. He took his hand away although he was still watching her. 'Which hotel are you staying at?' she asked, hoping her voice wasn't too obviously uneven.

'The GB.' He gestured over his shoulder at the Grande Bretagne, one of the best—and most expensive—hotels in Athens. 'I was reunited with my credit cards as well as my clothes in Crete,' he explained, reading her surprise without difficulty. 'Why don't you wait here and dabble your feet as planned? I'll be back in a couple of minutes.'

She watched as he walked towards the hotel, as relaxed and indifferent as any rich playboy on holiday, and wondered just what was going on. She really wasn't the sort of person to whom holiday romances happened. And she was a long way from certain that there was anything in the least romantic about her feelings for Craig. She was even less certain about his reasons for seeking her out. If he really had been repaying a debt, he was certainly overdoing it. Not that she minded. She grinned and slipped off her sandals to cool her toes in the fountain's tepid water as she thought about this sudden urge to take her photograph. A souvenir? Her smile faded. Souvenirs were of the past. It was as good a way as any, she supposed, of reminding her that today was not the beginning of anything; it was just a line drawn under a balance-sheet, that was all. She mustn't mistake charm for anything more substantial.

She was still telling herself that when she saw him crossing the road to rejoin her. Two scantily clad girls eating ice-cream looked up as he passed and exchanged giggling glances and Jane found herself irrationally annoyed, especially when Craig noticed and gave them a wide grin that redoubled their giggles and frankly admiring stares. She stood up, shaking the water from her feet. Souvenirs, she reminded herself firmly. That was all he wanted.

CHAPTER THREE

'WHAT happened to all the fancy gadgetry?' Jane wondered aloud as he approached. He held a small compact camera in one hand, but she observed that it had a far more complex-looking lens than her own relatively cheap camera.

'Fancy gadgetry has its own problems,' he told her and seemed to be wryly entertained by what was obviously a very private memory. He raised the small camera. 'Don't worry, this one is quite adequate.'

What had she been expecting: a studio session? All he wanted was a holiday snap, for heaven's sake. 'Where do you want me to pose?' she asked, suddenly self-conscious. She didn't consider herself particularly photogenic and this was beginning to seem like an awkward end to an enjoyable lunch. The sooner they got it over with, the better.

But it seemed that Craig had no intention of contenting himself with a single picture. He started to order her around with almost professional single-mindedness and it began to dawn on her that he actually intended to use up the whole reel of film.

'Haven't you finished?' she demanded after the first three or four shots. She was already regretting both agreeing to pose and the fact that her own camera was in the hotel. It would have been nice to have had at least one shot of him for her own souvenir—and she suspected that he *was* photogenic.

He ignored the plaintive note in her voice. 'I work on the principle that, if you take enough, one or two are bound to come out looking reasonable,' he told her, making a minute adjustment to the lens. 'Now, stand on the edge of that fountain and look cheerful.' He glanced from the viewfinder to her, vaguely exasperated. 'Well, take your shoes off again, you idiot! No one plays in fountains with their shoes on!'

Absurdly, she suddenly stopped being self-conscious and began to enjoy herself. If Craig wanted her to play around in the middle of the afternoon in central Athens, with tourists and pigeons looking distinctly puzzled all round her, then she was going to have fun. She laughed, and twirled dizzily in response to a curt gesture, letting him direct her as though he wanted her likeness from every possible angle. She perched on the stone wall beside the steps up to the road, leaning back in parody of more glamorous models, grinning at Craig's sudden chuckle of delight. It didn't matter what happened to the film or if every shot was blurred and unprintable, it was an extravagantly silly gesture on his part and it certainly transformed her idea of a rather drab and pathetic souvenir photo lying forgotten in some dusty drawer years from now.

She accepted all his instructions, letting him pose her alongside small children, and cats, and dust-bathing sparrows, and, finally, after her exhausted protests, in front of a large and opulent ice-cream.

He sat down opposite her, camera and jacket discarded on the seat beside him. 'You've got chocolate on your chin,' he observed critically, and leaned forward to wipe it off with his own white handkerchief.

It was the most casual of gestures, but somehow her breath had stopped in her throat. Long fingers held her chin in the lightest of holds, but her skin was scorched by his touch. Looking down, breathless, at the face which was so close to hers, intent on its task, she saw the fine lines of laughter or concentration which edged his eyes, the dusting of fair hair against the tanned complexion, the faint roughness where his beard would grow. The tips of his dark eyelashes had been bleached white by the sun, she noticed. Then he looked up and caught her gaze. For a long moment tension throbbed in the air between them and then, carefully, he let his hand drop and moved away.

'That's better.' His eyes still hadn't left hers and there was a curiously husky note in the light voice.

Sudden laughter from a group of schoolchildren passing by broke the spell. She could look away and take what felt like her first breath in minutes. Remotely, she saw that the hand with which she picked up her glass of iced water was not quite steady.

'Is the film finished?' she asked when she thought she could sound normal.

'Not quite.' His voice was dry, but there was no amusement in it.

She didn't want to pose again. She risked a glance at him. 'Do I get to take pictures of you?' she wondered. He might send her a copy, if she asked him.

He picked up the little camera, the moment of fleeting intensity gone. 'Do you know how to work this thing?'

'I press a button?' she hazarded, and was glad to hear his chuckle.

'Something like that. No, I've a better idea. Hang on.'

He walked quickly away towards two girls sitting at a nearby table. They were the same ones who had watched him earlier, she noticed, annoyance edging its way into her confused feelings. He bent over them, offering the camera and indicating Jane. She couldn't hear what he said, but they giggled again as he showed them the camera's mechanism.

As he returned to the table, the two girls with him, Jane waited, resigned. He held out a hand to her.

'Come on, darling, these two young ladies have agreed to take some shots of us together.'

The endearment, insincere though it obviously was, temporarily deprived her of speech. She let him tug her, without apparent effort, to her feet and did not even resist when he circled her waist with one arm, drawing her against him.

Still giggling, one of the girls lifted the camera and pressed the button. It whirred and clicked. Jane was quite ready to move away. Thin cotton clothes made a fragile barrier against the hard strength of his lean frame. He did not let her go. His arm tightened and he lifted his gaze from where it had rested with well-assumed affection on her and spoke to the girls.

'I think there are another four shots on the film,' Jane heard him say. 'Use them up while I take advantage of the situation.'

There was no time for her to do anything. She wasn't sure if she *could* have done anything. Later, she wasn't even sure if she had wanted to. The kiss on the boat hadn't prepared her. How could it? That had been hard and abrupt: an insult given and received. This was different.

He drew her into a closer embrace, his strength easily overcoming her initial resistance. And then she had let him lift her chin so that her face was turned up to his. It was all the opportunity he needed. Softly his lips touched her forehead and then, as her hands lifted tentatively to his shoulders, she saw him smile slightly, grey eyes narrowed and speculative, before his lips closed on hers and all coherent thought fled.

She had been kissed before. She was not entirely without experience. But nothing had prepared her for what flared between them as her lips parted beneath the gentle persuasion of his. The giggling girls, the camera, the tourists milling round them, all ceased to have any meaning. Reality was his body against hers, the surge and heat of excitement which swept through her as his hands tightened, and her own fingers twining in the fine hair that touched the back of his neck.

For a moment longer, the dizzying embrace continued and then, as if with infinite reluctance, his lips left hers, teasing them again quickly with a feather touch before his clasp loosened and he relaxed, holding her gently now, letting her lean against him as the blood began to pound less rapidly in her veins. Briefly she felt the brush of his cheek against her hair, then he lifted his head and spoke to the girls behind her. They weren't giggling any more and Jane decided that she had no wish to turn and see their expressions. She could feel the growing embarrassment in her own face.

'That's definitely adults only.' His voice sounded amused, but Jane could hear the rapid thud of his heart beneath her ear and had felt the fine tremor in the hand which had touched her hair. It was some comfort to know that he was almost as shaken as she had been by that kiss.

Still holding her, he reached out to retrieve the camera. He was laughing quietly now, whether at her or himself she couldn't tell. 'Thanks,' he said to the girls over her head and she heard footsteps clattering away, subdued murmurs retreating.

Carefully, giving her time to recover her poise, Craig stepped away before looking down at her. One glance was all she dared spare him. Remembered passion, her unqualified response to his touch, scorched her mind and her cheeks and she didn't ever want to meet his gaze again.

'Want to borrow these?' The despised sunglasses dangled in front of her, the enquiring voice blandly considerate. She looked at the glasses, and discovered she could still laugh. At once she felt better. She turned to him.

'Words fail me.' She gestured expressively.

'You need a drink.' The hand tucked under her arm as he led her to a seat in the shade was curiously impersonal. 'So do I,' he added, and there was a wryly surprised note in his voice.

For a few moments they both sat in silence. She couldn't read his thoughts—her own were in confusion. She wasn't even sure if she *liked* the man. He was certainly charming, and she enjoyed his company and shared his humour, but he was too well-armoured, too lacking in warmth. Or so she had thought. She did not know how to cope with passion, particularly not this unknown wildfire beyond her control. She did not *want* to cope with it.

His voice broke her train of thought. It was detached, almost rueful. 'I was right about you on that boat: you have hidden qualities. At the moment a certain rather powerful chemistry seems to be operating.'

Chemistry. That was one way of looking at it. It got you away from a few risky areas—like feelings. Did he have any? None that couldn't be brought under almost instant control, she decided, remembering that he too had felt that moment's passion.

She looked up. His light eyes held no readable expression and his mouth had that increasingly familiar upward tilt to one corner that was an invitation to share amusement. The long thin fingers were clasped loosely round a tall glass of beer, totally relaxed.

'In that case,' she managed coolly, choosing her words with painstaking detachment as though, she realised, she was carefully protecting a raw and aching wound from further hurt, 'I think we might as well cork up the bottle and replace it in whatever dark laboratory cupboard it came out of.' She was annoyed to hear the faint, be-traying edge which had crept into her voice.

'Shows how little you know about chemistry,' he commented carelessly. 'Confining an explosive reaction always makes it more intense,' he explained.

'Not if you keep the ingredients separate,' she pointed out.

'I think it's already too late for that.' He might have been as shaken as she at first; now she suspected he was enjoying the situation. The suspicion hardened her resolve.

'*Not* as far as I'm concerned.' This time she was pleased with the conviction in her voice. It came from a deep sense of self-preservation. She had no intention of flinging herself into some tawdry affair just because her hormones were suddenly being assertive. Besides, she reminded herself, the man was dangerous.

The smile creased his cheek. 'Coward,' he teased. His expression was quizzical as he watched the colour rise in her face. 'You may not like to acknowledge it,' he challenged her, 'but you can't pretend the chemistry isn't there.'

'Too bad,' she said curtly, irritation overcoming embarrassment. Why wouldn't he just drop the subject? He must realise she didn't want to discuss it. Then she looked up and saw that too-knowing smile on his face and her frayed temper gave. 'I've got a safe job, safe family and friends and that's how I like it,' she told him explosively. She wasn't going to storm out, but nor was she going to let him have the last word this time. 'I'm a teacher: practical, down-to-earth and security-minded. And it suits me.' Fleetingly, she wondered just how her friends, who had been so surprised when she'd decided to change jobs, would react to that claim. But even a desire for adventure had its very definite limits. His face showed only polite interest as she went on, 'And you could be a spy, a smuggler, a vagabond, or a con-man, for all I know—and I don't much care which. The answer's the same.' Short of breath, she stopped, reasonably pleased with the force of her rejection.

It didn't seem to have had much effect on Craig, who was leaning back in his chair, watching her. 'I wasn't proposing marriage,' he pointed out mildly.

'I wasn't accepting whatever sort of proposition you were making,' she retorted.

'Don't forget the chemistry.' He ran a long finger down the line of her jaw and, despite herself, she shivered in response before breaking away.

'Chemistry, as you've already noticed,' she snapped, 'isn't my subject.'

He chuckled. 'What *do* you teach? Infants?'

'No, adolescents.'

This time his laugh held real amusement and he raised a hand in a fencer's gesture, acknowledging a hit scored. Again, Jane realised how easy—and how dangerous—it would be to like him.

'All right. I apologise. I'll even send you copies of the photographs if you like. What's your address?'

She felt unexpectedly shy. She had hoped he would ask, but hadn't really believed he would. Then she realised that he still thought she was a teacher. Never mind. She took a scrap of paper from her bag and scribbled the school's address. If he really wanted to contact her, the school could pass on her new address; otherwise they could just forward the prints. If he sent them. After her outburst just now, there was no way she was going to explain about the very new and very speculative career in journalism that was just beginning.

As she handed the paper over, a rueful smile crossed her face. 'If any of the last few shots come out, I don't think I want to see them,' she decided.

He grinned. 'I thought you wanted one of me?' His soulful voice was openly provocative.

She did, but not one of those. 'If you've an old passport photo, I'd be glad of it,' she suggested.

'I'll see if I can get you the one off my prison ID card,' he offered, remembering her earlier comments on his background.

'I can just see you in prison clothes, with a convict haircut,' Jane agreed with enthusiasm. It was such a relief to be sparring at this superficial level again. Just now, she had almost been out of her depth.

She didn't have long to enjoy it, however. A few minutes later Craig looked at his watch and got to his feet, picking up the elegant jacket which gave the lie to her words and holding it casually over the shoulder of his fine cotton shirt.

'Business calls, unfortunately. I think the rest of this afternoon is going to seem remarkably dull. If I'm not arrested before then, I'll see you at the taverna at about nine, OK?'

'Fine,' she agreed automatically. Before she realised what he intended, he had lifted her hand from where it lay on the table and brushed her palm lightly with her lips.

'A salute to a model of surprising talents,' he told her ambiguously, and had walked off towards his hotel, leaving her sitting there, her hand clenched tightly in her lap, before she had a chance to think of anything at all to say. Then she realised that he had once again managed to have the last word, and couldn't help laughing aloud in her own salute to him. And he still intended to join her for dinner? She hadn't been convinced he'd meant it, particularly after what she'd just said to him. She'd be mad to go, of course; she'd learned that if she'd learned nothing else from the turmoil of the last hour. But why should she let a little thing like insanity stop her from doing something reckless? She hadn't done so far in her relationship with Craig Stanton.

People at neighbouring tables must already think her beyond salvation, she decided as she collected her belongings and began to make her way back to the hotel, totally unable to suppress the smile that kept forcing its way to her lips.

It was a few minutes before nine when she reached the restaurant, feeling as nervous as she had been when she was sixteen and on her first date with the boy who was captain of the school rugger team. That had been a disaster, she remembered wryly. At least this time she was old enough to take care of herself. With *Craig*? Her inner self was doubtful. Ruthlessly, she squashed the doubts. The evening would be fun; tomorrow she would fly back to England. And Craig Stanton would soon be nothing but a rather engaging memory of an entertaining end to a summer holiday. The inner voice remained sceptical, reminding her just how much control she had lost that afternoon, but she ignored it, looking at her surroundings with pleasure and shying away from a memory that was too uncomfortable to linger on. Particularly since its subject should arrive at any moment.

From the open-air restaurant—who would want to waste the warmth of a summer evening indoors?—she could look down over the roof's edge on the busy comings and goings at the stalls and shops in the street below. Nothing ever seemed to close. Less than a hundred yards away, the floodlit bulk of the Acropolis loomed over a scene it had guarded for thousands of years.

Thin cats, their careless grace irresistibly reminding her of Craig, strolled along the tiles of the parapet, weaving their way among the inevitable pots of basil and geraniums and eyeing the food being served while ignoring the perilous drop only inches away. A woman at a nearby table gave in and passed a chunk of meat to a slender tabby and Jane saw the titbit disappear avidly before the lucky animal sat back on its haunches to wait patiently for more.

'You encourage them,' Jane heard the man complain to his companion.

'They need it more than I do,' the plumpish woman replied.

'Well, tell them to keep their paws off my plate. Look at that!'

At first Jane thought his exclamation was directed at some flagrant exhibition of feline greed, but then she saw where he was pointing and leaned forward to see more clearly. From above she had a grandstand view.

'It's just some locals scuffling with the tourists,' decided the man's uninterested companion.

'I don't think so.' He spoke slowly. Something in his voice made Jane look more closely.

There was an almost menacing quality to the ugly little scene which was being enacted in the shadowed alleyway opposite, just a little distance from the crowded and brightly lit street. There seemed to be four men involved and Jane realised with rising indignation that it was not an evenly divided fight. Three of the men were apparently operating together against the fourth. It was an oddly unreal situation, like something from an old movie, and at first her anger was almost detached, directed against the general unfairness more than any personalities. But this was clearly not just a squabble over some insult, real or imagined. She spoke her thought aloud, sharply.

'Someone's going to get hurt!'

The three men were moving purposefully around the fourth, trying to ring him. He seemed to be attempting to keep the wall at his back while edging towards the light of the street. The fact that no blows had yet been exchanged only seemed to make it worse.

And then the situation changed abruptly. One of the three moved suddenly towards the victim and there was a blurred flurry of movement. The first man fell back a second later, clutching his wrist. He looked as though he was swearing quietly.

That was what was wrong, Jane realised. In a country where the mildest difference of opinion was conducted at full volume, this attack was taking place almost in silence. Things were moving faster now. The man against the wall was warding off kicks and punches from two directions and surely could not hope to hold out much longer, even though he was putting in some effective blows of his own. And then he was down. It was only for a second and then he was somehow back on his feet, but that second and the dim street lighting were all Jane needed.

She was running down the taverna stairs before her chair had clattered to the ground behind her or the other diners could complete startled exclamations. Outside, she looked around, her heart pounding in fear and rage. She needed help. The first man she saw was a Greek shopkeeper little older than herself. She grabbed his arm, ignoring his startled reaction.

'You must help!' she pleaded, hoping he spoke some, any, English. 'A fight!' She pointed desperately and then, to clinch it, 'My fiancé, he is hurt!'

The appeal to romance and chivalry worked faster than any fuller explanation could have done. He followed her as she released him to race down the alley. The man was still on his feet but his opponents were moving in again. Then one of them looked over his shoulder. Behind Jane he saw her Greek assistant, several other curious passers-by, and the couple from the restaurant. It was too much. He shouted something to his comrades and ran, closely followed by the others.

Shouts and gestures, but nothing else, pursued them. Jane spared one grateful smile for her champion and then was on her knees beside the figure who had slid down the wall to crouch, breathing heavily, against it. With an odd sense of *déjà vu*, she touched his shoulder.

'Are you all right?' She tried to sound neutral, hoping that nothing showed in her voice of the heart-stopping fear she had felt when he fell. Or the equally devastating wave of relief when his attackers had fled.

Craig looked up. There was blood on his face and he seemed dazed, but his eyes widened with recognition and a touch of resigned amusement the moment he saw her.

'I should have known. Can't you resist rescuing me?'

She tried to keep her own words light, stilling the tremor in her hands and subduing the urge to touch him again. If his voice was anything to go by, he was his usual, infuriating self.

'I'm trying to break the habit,' she managed drily, spoiling the effect by asking again, 'Are you all right?'

He stood up, stretching cautiously. 'I'm fine. Don't worry about me—I always come out on top.'

Relief allowed exasperation to flare. 'Like scum?' she suggested tartly. She pulled out her handkerchief. 'Here, borrow this. I think your nose is bleeding.' She took some pride in the fact that she did not flinch as she saw the damage more closely and that, whatever her internal

reaction to the sight of his blood, the hand that offered
the linen was steady.

He took it from her, the corner of his mobile mouth
lifting in what might even have been salute from a master
of self-control to a promising student. She thought he
was about to comment, but his attention was caught by
something the young Greek shopkeeper was saying. Craig
evidently had no trouble with the language because he
turned slowly back to Jane, an arrested expression on
his face.

'How long have we been engaged?' he asked mildly.

It wasn't fair that he could make her feel embarrassed
at her presumption even in this situation. 'I had to think
of *some* way to get help.' She wished she didn't sound
faintly apologetic and gestured to the smiling crowd
around them who seemed to think they had interrupted
a lovers' quarrel. 'It worked, didn't it?' she demanded,
slightly defensive.

'Undoubtedly.' His gaze followed hers and the
beaming faces smiled back at them both. Clearly the
quarrel was going to have a happy ending. The crowd
began to drift away. Her 'fiancé' turned back to her.

'I'm surprised you recognised me,' he remarked,
looking at their badly lit surroundings.

She pointed back to the taverna. 'I was watching from
the roof and when I saw you go flat on your back,
looking distinctly seedy, I knew you at once,' she told
him with some satisfaction.

He leaned back against the wall and laughed aloud.
'A truly memorable sight,' he chuckled. Then his voice
was for once serious, if rueful. 'I suspect that I really
do have to thank you this time. Three to one is always
easier in the movies than in real life. I'm sorry I spoiled
dinner,' he added.

'Don't mention it. I'll even promise not to hold you
to our engagement,' she offered.

'I'll have to think about that.' Humour was back in
his voice and he was looking at her in a way that made

her conscious of her flimsy cotton clothes. 'The prospect has unexpected possibilities.' Memories of that afternoon flared between them and she was the first to look away.

'Oh, no, it hasn't,' she told him firmly and stepped back.

'You've got blood on your skirt,' he noticed abruptly.

'Have I? It'll wash out.' It didn't seem to matter much. She surveyed him: his shirt had a tear in one sleeve and there was blood on it, dust marked his trousers and she didn't believe for a moment that he was as unaffected by the fight as he was pretending. She came to a decision whose wisdom she chose not to analyse. 'You look a mess. My hotel's much nearer than yours: you can borrow my bathroom to clean up and we can get a doctor to you if you need one. At least you won't have to shock the staff of the GB too much.'

'I doubt if they're shockable.' He looked down at himself and grimaced with distaste. 'I don't need a doctor, but you may be right about cleaning up—I don't think the taverna facilities are up to dealing with this.'

They walked back through the winding streets towards the hotel. Craig's appearance attracted one or two curious glances but, in a place that nightly saw the weirdest variety of human life, no one showed any real interest. If the thugs who'd attacked him were following him, Jane didn't notice: she was too concerned about her companion. He seemed to be walking without difficulty, though he had flinched slightly when she touched his left arm and she had quickly released him. His lips were thinned to a tight line and a slight frown narrowed his eyes. He either had a headache or was thinking hard. Perhaps both. At the moment he was very obviously the unresponsive 'John Smith' of the ferry, not the charming and eloquent companion of this afternoon.

At the hotel Jane reclaimed her key and Craig's battered state didn't earn even the flicker of an eyebrow. They jolted their way up to the sixth floor in the tiny lift and she went ahead to open the door to her room. It was only as she pushed it open, saying, 'Here we are,' that the first real doubts struck her.

The room, which only hours ago had seemed plain but adequate, now appeared stiflingly small, dominated by the presence of two single beds which left very little space for any sort of manoeuvring. Craig had followed her in and she heard the heavy click of the door shutting behind her.

Keep detached, she told herself, turning towards him. 'I'm afraid all I've got is some aspirin,' she said briskly, 'but the bathroom's all yours and there's usually plenty of hot water.'

'Aspirin will be fine; there's nothing seriously wrong,' he said almost indifferently, as though his thoughts were a long way off. Jane relaxed slightly, embarrassed by her own over-reaction, as she realised he was wholly unaware of the intimacy of the cluttered room. Then his expression lightened with a slightly lop-sided grin which had her pulse racing as though it were she, not he, who had been fighting. 'I seem to remember you feeding them to me once before,' he remembered.

'They worked then,' she said as drily as she could and then, needing to break the spell of the moment, picked up the clean towel left by the maid. 'Take this. The bathroom's behind the door you're leaning against and the aspirin are on the shelf in there.'

He caught the towel one-handed. 'Thanks. I'll see what I can do about the wreckage.'

Jane heard the sound of water running and a muffled comment that might have been an oath. Did he need help? She wondered if he was more badly hurt than he had appeared, and found herself listening hard in case he fell. Then her treacherous mind was replacing images of his injuries with a vision of his lean body, with its narrow hips and surprisingly strong shoulders, beneath the shower, and she found herself flushing at the direction of her unruly thoughts. Safe, practical Jane

Simpson didn't indulge in that sort of fantasy, she reminded herself sharply, ignoring the tendency of her more reckless side to do exactly that.

For the sake of something to occupy her, she examined the damage to her own clothes: a spot or two of blood and a considerable amount of dust on her skirt. Nothing to worry about. The water was still running in the bathroom and it didn't take a minute to swap the skirt for the cotton trousers she'd been wearing when he had first turned up at the door of her room. Somehow it seemed impossible that that had been only this morning. And that that had been only the second time in her life she had met Craig Stanton. She smiled wryly at her reflection in the mirror and tugged a comb through her fair curls. Heaven alone knew what any further meeting might bring.

The sound of splashing had ceased and a minute later she heard the bathroom door open. Almost reluctantly, she turned to face him and was relieved to discover that he was at least wearing his trousers even though he was carrying his shirt over one arm. He hung it on the wardrobe door and she realised that he had rinsed out the patches of blood. She wasn't quite sure what to say. The sight of his flatly muscled chest and the light sprinkling of hair tapering towards his belt made her mouth suddenly dry. Mocking herself, she decided that her imagination was clearly wholly inadequate. She had not known a naked chest could have this effect on her—after all, she'd seen plenty on the beaches recently and none of them had induced this imbecilic response.

Her silence must have struck him as uncharacteristic because he lifted a quizzical eyebrow. 'Are you OK?' he wondered. 'No delayed shock?'

Not from the fight, anyway. She shook her head. 'No. What about you? How much did they really hurt you? I'm sure I saw a boot or two go in.'

'They did their best,' he agreed, 'but I've only a couple of bruises and a cut on one arm to show for it. There's no real damage—you and the Seventh Cavalry got there in time.'

'I'm glad to hear it.' She hoped her voice didn't reflect the rather hollow feeling in her stomach at the sight of the narrow gash on his left forearm. 'You make a lousy invalid.'

He chuckled at the memory, his grin unrepentant. 'Don't you?'

She had to laugh. It was true. 'I'm awful. I swear at everyone for fussing and then, when I'm left alone. I grumble about being neglected.' She saw him pick up his shirt as though checking whether it was still too damp to wear. 'Leave that. I've a travel iron that'll dry it out. Let me put something on your arm.'

'Still playing Florence Nightingale?' he wondered without much enthusiasm.

'If you're still in the wars, why not?' She rummaged in her half-packed case and found a dressing and a light bandage. 'At least this will stop you getting blood all over your shirt again.'

He held out his arm but she thought he seemed reluctant to allow even this much attention to his wound. It wasn't serious, she was relieved to see. She didn't know much about first aid and was discovering that it was possible to feel quite as ill as the person you were treating. Aware of the warmth of his flesh so close to her, feeling his eyes on her head as she bent over her task, she found touching him unexpectedly difficult. She was glad to fasten the small safety pin and step back.

'There, that should do.' Her voice was breathy and it was her pulse, not his, that was racing. She moved self-consciously away from the bed he was sitting on, busying herself needlessly tidying a few scattered objects. 'What was it all about, anyway?' she finally couldn't help asking. So much for not showing too much curiosity.

From the corner of his eye she saw him shrug, then wince. 'Couple of muggers, or someone feeling rather anti-tourist?' The tone was dismissive, indifferent.

Another no-go area, it seemed. Why? She wasn't going to let him leave it at that. Any normal person would surely be clamouring for the police or a doctor, if not both.

'There were three of them, and they seemed to know exactly what they were doing,' she persisted.

'Well, they'd obviously left you out of their calculations,' he retorted. 'So had I,' he added almost ruefully, but the amusement seemed more like an attempt to deflect the subject and this time she didn't intend to be shut out. She turned to him.

'A good thing, wasn't it? Don't you think you owe me some sort of explanation? And don't mention muggers again, because I don't believe in them any more than you do,' she told him bluntly.

He stood up, reaching for his shirt and shrugging into it, ignoring the damp patches on sleeve and collar and the pain the action must have cost him. He stared at her as he buttoned it, his eyes arctic and his mouth a harder line than any she had yet seen. 'You have no idea what I believe. And I don't owe you anything. You chose to interfere—again—and if you can't live with the consequences, then that's entirely your problem. I recommend that you find someone a little more impressionable to play nanny to next time. I'm sorry about dinner, but somehow I don't feel in the mood any more. Enjoy your flight tomorrow.' He bent and picked up his jacket from the bed.

She felt sick. It was as though he'd become a total stranger—not 'John Smith,' not Craig, just a hostile man who couldn't wait to be rid of an interfering acquaintance who had the conceit to think two meetings constituted a relationship. For a moment, tears blurred her eyes. No, she wasn't going to cry.

'I'm sorry,' she managed. 'Next time. I'll ignore you.'

'There won't be a next time.' His voice was final, absolute. She shouldn't have given him the chance but he hadn't had to be so brutal. At least it gave her back some badly needed self-control.

'Naturally not,' she agreed as coolly as she could. Why didn't he just go? His hand, with those long fingers that had held her so tenderly, was on the door-handle. 'Goodbye,' she said clearly, and turned her back.

'Goodbye.' She heard the door open, then he must have hesitated and she turned again to see him reach into his jacket pocket. He tossed a small parcel on to the rumpled bed. 'I bought that for you.' The edge of ice in his voice thawed fractionally.

Then the door had closed behind him and she was alone in the suddenly empty room. She fumbled at the little package. A finely woven scarf of clear blue cotton, its edges trimmed with golden sequins, tumbled on to her lap. It was only then that she gave up trying to be calm and controlled and allowed the floodgates of misery and disillusion to open.

CHAPTER FOUR

ENGLAND'S summer was drawing to its close. Jane had managed to paint most of the studio flat in Islington, and now it was beginning to feel like home. She had been back for over a week and two days of acute depression had been followed by frantic activity that not only improved her surroundings dramatically but was also at least partly successful in keeping her mind off Craig Stanton and his effect on her. If she hadn't yet found a way to keep him out of her dreams, well, surely even they would fade eventually? It wasn't as though anything had really happened, after all. When she got to that stage in her musings, she would wonder just who she was trying to fool and either go out and buy more paint or retreat downstairs hoping to be distracted by Sally's gossip.

It had been that impulse which had led to one more discovery about Craig. Sally was a disorganised art student whose occasional evening celebrations made Jane's room vibrate to the beat of their music. After spending one evening trying to ignore it, and having discovered that Sally used the leftovers from each party to stock her eccentric pantry, she had collected a quiche and a bottle of cheap wine and gone downstairs to join in. Sally's general goodwill and cheerfulness made Jane more than willing to put up with the occasional disturbed evening and, anyway, she had already discovered that writing was far more solitary than teaching. Sally was good company.

She had paid a visit one afternoon not long after she began the orgy of decorating and, over black coffee out of chipped mugs, had found herself telling her new friend about her recent holiday—including a strictly edited

version of the encounter with Craig. The absurdly
anonymous name and the luxurious lunch had stayed in;
the chemistry had been carefully omitted. She had briefly
mentioned the photography session in Syntagma Square
and it was at that point that Sally's brow had creased
in concentration.

'Just a moment. Did you say this guy's called Craig
Stanton and was loaded with cameras?' she demanded.

Puzzled, Jane nodded. 'That's right. Have I missed
something?'

Sally got up. 'I think you just might have. Here, take
a look at this.' She rummaged in a heap of books stacked
on the floor and found a large, slender volume which
she handed to Jane without further comment.

She took it, looking down at the stark black and white
picture on the glossy cover. *Voyages*, it was called. She
opened it and slowly began leafing through a sequence
of unforgettable images. It was a visual account of one
man's travels from glossy California to the slums of
India. But it was far more than a book of travel photographs. It was almost a pilgrimage. Beneath the glitter
of Los Angeles, the sleaze lurked; behind the abject
poverty of Calcutta was a proud Indian culture. There
were few captions or titles: none was necessary. Whoever
had taken these pictures had the insight of an artist as
well as the detachment of a surgeon in his merciless
exposure of the hypocrisies of the rich and the dignity
of the poor.

Jane knew nothing about photography, but she felt
she would have wanted to know the creator of these
images. If she hadn't already met him. She looked again
at the name in small letters on the title page: Craig
Stanton. His own picture inside the back of the dust-
jacket only confirmed what she had recognised as a certainty from the moment she received the book from
Sally's hands. It explained the hint of familiarity about
the name, and the fact that he had looked as though he

thought she might recognise it. It also made everything else about him even more confusing.

She looked at the book in her hands again before meeting Sally's expectant gaze. 'I knew he was interested in photography,' she admitted. 'I never dreamt he was a professional.'

'He's more than that: he's an artist.' Sally sounded more than usually emphatic. 'Did he really take pictures of you?' she demanded eagerly, a note of envy in her voice.

'A whole reel.' For some reason, that memory now seemed faintly depressing. Had he just been mocking her ignorance, knowing she would eventually discover his identity? Had there even been a film in the camera? she wondered.

'That's fantastic! Is he going to give you copies?'

'I doubt if I'll ever hear from him again,' she told her friend flatly, remembering their parting. 'He probably won't even bother to process the film.'

Sally looked totally unbelieving and began demanding more details of the encounter, so that eventually Jane made an excuse and left. She had less desire than ever to discuss her fleeting acquaintance with Craig Stanton. The visit to Sally had done nothing at all to distract her errant thoughts.

After that, the work with both paintbrush and typewriter proceeded with even more intensity. One afternoon, however, she allowed herself to be lured out by unexpected sunshine and an urge to explore the neighbourhood. At first it was fun. She decided to walk home through the park and it was here that something happened which dampened her enthusiasm for solitary walks.

It was quite late in the afternoon by then and there were few people around. She sat for a while on a bench, but that allowed too many unwanted thoughts to surface and she began to walk briskly homewards. It was as she did so that she began to feel uneasy. In a park so nearly deserted, it was odd that someone should be echoing her random movements. It must be her imagination, she decided. But she quickened her step anyway, trying not to glance too obviously towards the slight, dark-haired man who seemed more interested in her than in the scenery. Suddenly, the empty park wasn't nearly so inviting. She wasn't far from the gates and the street outside looked reassuringly busy. Then, with safety in sight, her habitual defiance asserted itself. It was, after all, almost certainly all in her mind, the product of too many warnings about the dangers of London and reading too many thrillers. There was another seat not far away and she deliberately sat on it, apparently absorbed in watching the progress of some ducks waddling across the grass.

Thirty yards away, the man stopped, bending to tie a shoelace and then taking a letter from his pocket and consulting it. Coincidence? It wasn't just the evening chill which made Jane shiver, feeling a moment of near-panic. Imagination or not, common sense told her not to be a fool. She walked fast to the exit and didn't linger on the rest of the short journey home. She didn't even look behind her until she arrived, breathless and flushed, at her own front door. Never had its peeling paint seemed more welcoming.

It had all been too hopelessly vague to report to the police and she didn't know what else to do about it. What made her even more uncomfortable was the feeling which haunted her that she had seen the man before. Had there been someone like him on the bus the previous day? But it was more than that—she had noticed the man on the bus because there was something elusively familiar about him. She tried to dismiss it from her mind, but she also cut down on solitary walks and concentrated instead on redecorating the flat.

By the time it was done she was tired but triumphant. It was as though she could now really get on with her fresh start. She supposed she ought to go out and celebrate, but there was something very appealing about just sitting back to admire her own handiwork. She would buy some wine and persuade Sally to come up for lunch if she was in.

Twenty minutes later she arrived back from the corner shop and knocked on Sally's door. 'Lunch?' she offered, lifting the bottle in invitation. Sally's expression startled her: she looked both impressed and envious. 'What's wrong?' Jane asked. 'Don't you want my lunch?'

'Nothing's wrong at all,' Sally told her, beginning to smile and opening the door a little wider. 'I'll even relieve you of the wine, since I gather you're going out.'

'I am? What on earth do you mean?' Intrigued and amused, Jane handed over the bottle and stepped into the living-room of the small flat. Whatever Sally was going to say in explanation faded at once into silence as Craig got lazily up from the chair in which he had been lounging.

'Craig?' Her voice was barely a whisper. The uncontrollable surge of unmixed delight that she felt as she saw him confused and startled her. She should be furious with him. She wasn't. 'What are you doing here?' she asked in a more normal tone.

'Waiting for you.' Whatever her reaction to him, it was clearly one-sided. Her own smile faded and she stopped her impulsive move towards him as she registered the curt tone of his words. 'There are things we have to talk about.'

'Are there? I thought we'd sorted everything out already,' she reminded him. Behind her, she could sense Sally's avid curiosity, but she couldn't take her eyes from Craig. He was looking fit and as elegant as ever. His eyes, however, were the grey of a winter sea and everything about him suggested someone doing a job that was at best boring and probably tiresome too. She began to wish he'd stayed away.

'Not quite,' he was saying. 'Something's come up.'

And it was obviously a nuisance. She knew him well enough to know that just telling him that it was his problem and that he could go away wouldn't work. Besides, she also knew herself well enough to know exactly what any such reaction would do to her own curiosity. He might even leave just to irritate her into following. Then she realised what else he had said and she couldn't help the slow smile. 'Craig, are you saying that you've actually gone to the trouble of finding me in order to *discuss* something?'

Her unconcealed incredulity, the reminder of their previous row, was not without its effect. The indifference melted as his lips twitched and she saw the glint of appreciative laughter in his eyes. 'The age of miracles has arrived,' he admitted.

She chuckled. 'You'd better come up to my flat so that you can tell me all about it,' she decided. 'I hope you don't mind the smell of paint.'

'I'm not keen on it. Anyway, there's someone we have to meet for lunch, so you might as well come straight over to my place—there's something there I need to show you.'

The photographs? Something in the set of his thin face told her he wasn't going to answer that question. She glanced down at her cheerful yellow tracksuit. 'I'll change,' she decided. 'Sally will keep you entertained. She's a fan,' she added drily.

It didn't seem to bother him that she had found out who he was. He sat down again and looked around the room. 'I'll wait,' he agreed and then, in a much more charming voice, asked Sally, 'Are you an art student? Where are you studying?'

Jane closed the door carefully on the sound of her friend's enthusiastic chatter and went thoughtfully upstairs to her own room. As she took a natural linen skirt and coral-coloured shirt from her wardrobe, her thoughts were more on Craig than on what she was wearing.

Whatever crazy reaction she might have had when she saw him, he clearly wasn't here because he wanted to see her again. Until that last moment of humour, he might have been 'John Smith' on the ferry again. But obviously *something* had made him go to the trouble of discovering her whereabouts from the school. Did he know that she'd left there permanently? she wondered. She fastened the wide leather belt round her narrow waist and quickly applied mascara and lipstick, glad that her tan still showed despite the days of working inside. There was one advantage to going anywhere with Craig, she reflected ruefully as she made her way back downstairs, since he'd seen her on the ferry: every appearance after that had to be an improvement.

He was silent as they left the building together. He must have called for a taxi from Sally's, Jane realised, because one was waiting for them. He held the door for her and gave the driver a Chelsea address.

'When did you get back to England?' she asked, since he didn't seem inclined to be communicative.

'Ten days ago,' he told her readily enough, but she had the impression his thoughts were miles away. They might have been two strangers exchanging polite conversation, Jane thought. And then remembered that they *were* little more than strangers, however strongly she had reacted to him since she had first seen him on the boat. He knew a little about her; she knew even less about him. But that wasn't entirely true, either. She did not understand him; there were mysteries about him that baffled and infuriated her, but on another level she felt she knew him well, and he too often seemed to know and understand exactly what she was thinking.

'No more questions?' The lightly mocking voice interrupting her thoughts was provocative.

'Not yet,' she warned him. 'I'm just enjoying the prospect of this talk you've promised me. Although I *am* curious about how you found me,' she confessed, and was encouraged by the spontaneous chuckle which greeted the admission.

'Not easily. Getting information out of that school is as bad as infiltrating MI5. I ended up using my best Texan drawl and pretending to be your stepfather.'

She shot him a suspicious glance but his expression was unreadable. She wasn't *quite* convinced that he was joking, but they had arrived at an attractive mews house in a quiet cul-de-sac and the taxi was stopping.

Craig paid the driver and unlocked the dark blue front door. 'Upstairs.' He gestured to the stairs which led up one side of the long hall. A closed door to her right intrigued her. Was that where he did his photographic work?

On the first floor a wide living-room spanned the whole front of the house. It was a long, lofty room, full of light and both comfortable and uncluttered. An antique sofa table and some graceful armchairs contrasted happily with a modern settee which invited total relaxation with its unashamed opulence. The pictures on the wall were equally varied—both old and modern—but there were no photographs among them. Lack of conceit, or lack of interest?

'My own pictures are upstairs,' he said, watching her, a current of humour in his voice. Blast him, was her expression really as revealing as all that? 'I'll add a couple of you some time,' he promised.

This time he *had* to be joking. 'No chance,' she declined brusquely. 'I'm no model.' It was embarrassing to find herself remembering his description of her as a 'model of surprising talents' and wished heatedly that either her memory was less accurate, or that her delicate complexion didn't flush so easily. She didn't give him a chance to exploit her comment. 'What was it you wanted to tell me about?' she asked instead.

Any humour that he might have been finding in the situation evaporated at once. She found herself thinking that he looked tired as well as irritable. At a gesture from him, she sat in one of the armchairs. He stared moodily at her for a moment as though she was an unwanted problem before dropping heavily into a chair opposite her.

'Why the *hell* did you leave that school?' he demanded.

It was the last thing she had expected to hear. 'What do you mean? What on earth does it matter to you what I do with my life?' she protested.

'In general terms, I don't give a damn whether you run a circus or the United Nations—I'm sure you'd do either equally well and I doubt if there's much difference between them,' he added, his voice fractionally milder. He ran his hand through his hair in a gesture she found achingly familiar. 'Just now, however, it's an infernal complication.'

'Why?' Her voice stayed cool but her bewilderment was growing rapidly. Any lingering hope that he might have had some remotely personal interest in her was perishing with humiliating speed. 'You're going to have to tell me all about it, aren't you?' she realised with compensatory satisfaction.

'I'll tell you what I have to, that's all,' he corrected. He hesitated, as if wondering where to begin, then said, 'You remember the state I was in when I was on the ferry?' She nodded. 'That was because I'd just spent several days trying to avoid those thugs who attacked me in Athens.' She was shocked, but a quick glance from those chilly eyes stilled her instinctive protest. She'd asked for an explanation, hadn't she? She couldn't complain if she didn't like it. 'I've been travelling rather widely in the Middle East lately,' he went on. 'My publishers are keen for a new book on the subject.' He looked enquiringly at her as though to check how much she already knew.

'I've seen *Voyages*,' she told him.

'So you know the sort of thing. What you don't know is that, for one reason or another, I sometimes combine my travels with some odd jobs for a friend of my father's.' Who had been in the diplomatic service, she recalled. This was beginning to sound more dramatic than anything she had imagined and she wasn't at all sure that she wanted to be involved. Apparently, however, it was too late. He shrugged at her expression. 'Nothing particularly glamorous—it's usually a question of delivering or collecting some information. Just occasionally, Toby asks me to point the camera in a direction that's not officially approved.'

Even put like that, it sounded dangerous. 'And this was one of those occasions?' If her tone was dry that was because her mouth felt parched. It was all right to read about such things in thrillers: real life was something else entirely.

'Just so.' The twist to his mouth held absolutely no humour at all. 'Only this time I wasn't quite discreet enough and someone spotted what I was up to.'

'Oh, dear.' It wasn't exactly adequate, but it was hard to think of something appropriate when your stomach seemed to have disappeared entirely.

'Quite. I didn't feel like spending several years in a Middle Eastern gaol trying to convince my captors of the purity of my motives so I chose to leave the region rather less legitimately than I had entered it. What I hadn't bargained on was how determined the pursuit would be. I managed to cross Turkey and get to Kos, but somewhere in one of my less wholesome resting places I was obviously bitten by something my system disliked—hence the fever. You know all about that,' he reminded her unnecessarily.

'Yes, but…' She hesitated, wondering if she was being an idiot.

'What?' He sounded resigned, but at least he was answering her questions.

'In Athens,' she began, 'you seemed, well, much more relaxed than on the boat. At first, anyway,' she amended, remembering the fight and the scene which had followed.

He seemed irritated again. 'You don't think I'd have looked you up if I thought I was still being followed, do you?' Obviously only a moron would have thought any such thing.

'How should I know? I've never met a spy before,' she protested, annoyed by his tone.

He chuckled. 'A very part-time and amateur spy. And not very efficient, it seems,' he added, sobering. 'No, I saw no one unusual on the ferry—except you.' However ambiguous that comment was, Jane couldn't help enjoying it. But he still hadn't explained why he had sought her out. Then she remembered his mention of repaying debts, and felt less cheerful. 'I thought I must have got rid of the pursuit and it wasn't until that attack that I realised they were still after me.'

'I still don't see how this concerns me,' Jane said slowly, not at all sure that she wanted to know any of this. 'I mean, I'm glad to know why you were being so uncommunicative in Athens...' his smile twisted at the memory but she went on with determination '...but presumably you've got rid of the wretched pictures to your friend Toby by now, so it's all over. Isn't it?' she ended on a note of doubt.

He stood up as though the situation was too infuriating to allow him to sit still. 'Of course I've handed over the photos and yes, it ought to be over, but it's not that simple. This arrived two days ago.'

He walked over to a small bureau and took an envelope from its top drawer, handing it to her. 'This' contained a sheet of cheap, yellowish paper. '"You and your accomplice will suffer for your spying",' she read aloud. The threat and the unevenly cut out pieces of newspaper which formed the letters were such a cliché that, at first, it was almost comic. But it was also real. 'Is this serious?' she demanded incredulously, dropping the paper with distaste on to the table by her chair. Disgust and anger prevented fear from touching her for the moment.

'I don't know,' he admitted. The simple statement was somehow almost more disturbing than anything else. For once in her acquaintance, he wasn't pretending.

'They've followed you to England?' He nodded, watching her as the implications of the nasty little note sank in. 'And they think *I'm* your accomplice?' she realised with rising indignation.

'Your heroic defence of me in Athens proved it, I should think,' he told her wryly.

'Next time, the thugs can keep you. What are you going to do about this?' What could he do? She could see that he couldn't go to the police, but suddenly her safe world was a frightening place.

'While I thought you were living at a girls' boarding school there wasn't much problem. I knew you were there even in the holidays...' she was surprised he had remembered something she only recalled mentioning briefly on the ferry—and she hadn't thought he was listening '...and it's a pretty contained set-up there. Middle Eastern muggers wouldn't find it easy to be unobtrusive in rural Hertfordshire and one of Toby's friends could have kept a discreet eye on things until it was all over. *Then* I discover you've thrown all that in and have moved to London.' He sounded irritated, as though she had ruined a perfectly good plan, which was very unfair. He didn't, however, give her a chance to say so. 'That's why you and I are going to have lunch with Toby: he claims to have an idea that will sort things out.' If tone of voice was anything to go by, Craig was less optimistic than his friend.

Jane wanted to protest that she didn't need or want protection and that she'd be glad if they would leave her out of their game of spies when the anonymous letter caught her eye again. She looked up. Craig read her expression without difficulty.

'Too late. You're already involved,' he reminded her unsympathetically.

'I'm just beginning to realise that,' she admitted reluctantly. 'I'm not sure I want any lunch, but perhaps I had better meet your friend.'

'Lunch and Toby go together. Come on.' He bent to pick up the tan leather jacket he had dropped on a chair as he entered the room. As he straightened, she must have revealed something of her uncertainty because he held out a hand to help her up and said, in a much less neutral voice, 'Don't worry. No one's going to harm you.'

Stupid tears prickled her eyelids. She sniffed. 'Of course not. I just wish I'd done a more thorough job in Athens.' She hoped she sounded a little more positive than she felt.

He laughed. 'You didn't do badly—I was glad to be on your side. Come on,' he repeated, 'we'll take a taxi, then we'll be harder to follow.' Somehow, that wasn't entirely comforting, Jane decided as she went downstairs with him.

Toby's club was old-fashioned, mahogany-panelled, and quiet. Craig was greeted with deferential familiarity by the steward, Jane with altogether more reserve. 'The last bastion of chauvinism,' he agreed cheerfully, interpreting her expression without difficulty. 'Toby's in the Ladies' Dining-Room—we'll have the place to ourselves, I expect.'

Jane looked around at the funereal surroundings. 'I believe you. I can't imagine there's a queue of ladies wanting to get in,' she decided, half hoping the steward was still within earshot.

'Behave,' she heard Craig mutter without much conviction, as he led her across the large room to a man in late middle-age who had stood up as they entered. He was tall and florid-faced and beginning to put on weight and Jane wondered whether, without Craig's information, she would have missed the shrewd intelligence in the pale blue eyes. 'Jane, may I introduce Colonel Toby Carstairs? Toby, this is Jane Simpson.'

Toby took her hand and smiled warmly. 'I'm delighted to meet you, Miss Simpson, despite the circumstances. Perhaps we can talk business after we've eaten, eh?'

It was an instruction, not a request, but he was the only one who did any justice to the roast meat, or to the trifle which followed. The conversation was formal and trivial and, by the time they adjourned for coffee to the relative comfort of the small annexe to the dining-room, the whole business was beginning to seem unreal. The abrupt change of tone when Craig next spoke, however, altered that.

'Do you really have a plan?' he demanded, not sounding particularly hopeful.

'Oh, yes,' the older man agreed coolly, taking his time over lighting his pipe. 'And I don't suppose you'll think much of it.'

'As usual. What's the difficulty about keeping Jane safe?'

'What about you?' she worried. 'You're in more danger than I am, surely?' That his thoughts seemed to be entirely of *her* safety was something to be savoured later; at present she was concerned for both of them.

'The problem,' said Toby, interrupting ruthlessly and without effort, 'is that we've looked at the Islington place and there's no way we can make it secure.'

Jane wondered uncomfortably who the 'we' were who had investigated her flat. Then she realised something else, and immediately felt relieved. 'So it was your men lurking in the park the other day?' she assumed.

Both Toby and Craig looked surprised. Toby shook his head. 'No. Craig only managed to find out where you were late yesterday.' The blue eyes narrowed. 'Why do you ask?'

Feeling rather as though she was making a fuss about nothing, Jane explained what had happened. Neither man showed any inclination to tell her she was imagining things.

'You said the man seemed vaguely familiar?' Craig asked. 'Can you describe him?'

'I'm hopeless on faces,' she admitted, then saw the quiet insistence on his. She concentrated, trying to remember. 'He was quite slight, sallow-skinned,' she recalled. 'He had a moustache and dark hair.' Craig was watching her closely as she searched her memory. Perhaps it was that that suddenly focused the man's image in her mind. 'Oh no!' she realised with a sudden sense of horror. Events hadn't been completely real until now.

'What's wrong?' That was Toby, but she was staring at Craig, her expression revealing as she relived that scene in Athens.

'I think Jane's just remembered that the last time she saw this man she was pursuing him down an alley in Athens. Am I right?' Craig suggested.

Jane nodded. He *had* been one of those three thugs. 'It was just that the light was so bad when I first saw him—that was why I didn't recognise him. But I still don't understand. *Why* are they still bothering you now? Us,' she corrected grimly.

'Craig has a theory that it's not all of them,' Toby told her when Craig said nothing. 'He thinks that most of them have given up but that one of them has taken it all personally and is conducting his own private vendetta out of some sort of wounded pride. Hence the anonymous note. And I,' he admitted as Craig seemed about to say something, 'can't think of a better explanation. Still, if there's only one of them, we should be able to flush him into the open quite easily.'

'Is that a good thing?' In this old-fashioned room with its quietly ticking clock and chintz-covered furniture, it all seemed slightly grotesque, but she wasn't sure she liked that 'we' any better than the earlier one.

From Craig's expression, he wasn't happy either. 'You still haven't said what you intend to do to protect Jane. Isn't there somewhere safe——?'

'Possibly,' Toby interrupted again. 'The best place I can think of is that house of yours in Chelsea.'

'*What?*' Toby smiled benevolently as two voices spoke in horrified chorus.

'You're mad.' Craig's voice was flat with disbelief. 'It not only puts her right in the middle of all the trouble, it also confirms their idea that she's my "accomplice".'

Jane thought shock had numbed her feelings, until she heard the rest of Toby's suggestion. 'Not if you're engaged to be married,' he said, as though presenting the most logical argument possible.

The whole world had clearly run mad. Toby was suggesting the impossible as though it were wholly reasonable and her own heart had leaped absurdly at the suggestion as though, for one crazy moment, she had actually wanted some part in this lunacy. But there was still one certainty left if self-preservation had any say in the matter. At least indignation was a good substitute for other, less manageable feelings.

'I don't want to get engaged. I don't want to live with anyone. And,' she added with cold certainty and as much control as a fast-disappearing temper would allow, 'the last person in the world I would want to be engaged to or live with is Craig. Is that clear?'

He was evidently in a similar state. 'Quite clear. And if it's any consolation, your feelings are shared. I've an exhibition to prepare and a terrorist breathing down my neck, and the last thing I intend to do is allow myself to be saddled with an inquisitive ex-teacher with a Florence Nightingale complex who can't keep out of trouble for five minutes.'

'I managed quite well till I met you,' she snapped, 'and you're not exactly a trouble-free zone yourself as far as I can see. No one's attacked me yet and I think I'd prefer to rely on my *friends* to help me if I need it,' she added with deliberate emphasis.

'No man in his right mind would make friends with you,' he retorted. Why should that comment hurt? They were flinging every insult that came to hand and she doubted if the sedate little room had ever heard such raised voices before.

They both became aware at the same time of Toby watching them with amused interest. 'And you can stop smirking,' Craig told him coldly. 'This has to be your craziest idea yet. I am not, repeat *not*, going to get engaged just to fit in with one of your lunatic schemes.'

Toby cleared his throat, improbably sounding slightly hesitant. 'My I ask if—er—Jillian is the problem?'

Craig looked taken aback, then dismissively impatient. 'Of course not. That was months ago.'

Was it? Jane quietly stored the name away in her memory. She had always known there must be some woman, perhaps several, in Craig's background. Toby looked as though he was waiting to hear her objections. She tried to sound reasonable.

'I left teaching because I wanted to be independent. I certainly don't want to move out of my new home, and anyway,' she added impulsively, looking at Craig who had stood up and was staring down into the empty fireplace, 'no one in their right minds would ever believe we were engaged. I'm just not his type.'

He looked up at that, the thunderous expression lifting, and for a moment the grey eyes sparkled. 'Oh? What *is* my type?' he challenged softly.

Because it was something she had tormented herself with on too many sleepless night, it didn't take much thought. 'Tall, slender, sophisticated, elegant,' she listed unemotionally. Everything, in fact that she wasn't. It was a depressing thought.

Head on one side, he was considering the catalogue. 'Sounds expensive,' he decided.

'You would know,' she pointed out.

Infuriatingly, he nodded, his smile irritatingly reminiscent. 'I do.' She wanted to throw something, then he added quietly, 'But you've forgotten the chemistry.'

She felt scarlet scald her face. She had forgotten nothing; now it seemed that neither had he.

Toby's impatient voice broke the tension that had begun to stretch between them. 'You're missing the point.' They weren't. Chemistry was the reason that she had no intention of staying anywhere with Craig Stanton, but she wasn't going to tell Toby that. Reluctantly she looked away from the challenge in Craig's eyes and towards the older man. 'No one's actually asking you to get *married*,' he was explaining, 'and engagements can be broken any time. All we need is for you two to stay together to make it easier to protect you both and to find the man who's after you.' Jane had an uneasy feeling that his order of priorities placed the latter target first. By the fireplace, Craig was still stiff with rejection of the whole idea.

'There has to be a better way,' he insisted.

'There isn't,' Toby told them flatly. 'Besides, aren't you forgetting something?'

'What?' Craig was impatient, almost preoccupied, and Jane could sense that he was searching hard for an alternative. She found she had clenched her hands tightly in her lap and carefully forced them to straighten. It dawned on her that she didn't even know if she wanted him to find a way out. She knew what she ought to be wishing for.

Toby's bland voice was smoothly reminiscent. 'You told me about the Athens fight—I remember it made quite a good story. Certainly made me want to meet you, Miss Simpson,' he added with a nod to her.

'You'd better call me Jane,' she said resignedly. Had her blundering intervention kept the whole Foreign Office entertained?

Craig was staring at Toby, an almost unwilling smile tugging at his mouth. Toby saw it, and nodded. 'That's right, my boy. You already *are* engaged, aren't you?' he asked Jane.

CHAPTER FIVE

IN THE taxi on the way to buy the ring, they were still arguing.

'It's not my fault. You shouldn't have told Toby what I said,' Jane pointed out unsympathetically.

'It was your idea in the first place,' he reminded her.

'Yes, and I said I wouldn't hold you to it.' Another grievance surfaced. 'Do we really have to get a ring?'

'Do you have one that will do?' They had been through this already. He knew very well that she had nothing even remotely appropriate and she knew there was no point in this farce of an engagement if it wasn't public. They had to have a ring. 'What have you got against marriage anyway?' he wondered. 'Not to me,' he added quickly, 'just in general.'

For a moment she imagined marriage to Craig: dizzying excitement, passion beyond the edge of control, moments of laughter and breathtaking intimacy. She could imagine all those, and she was not going to pretend to herself that they, and Craig, didn't have an almost overwhelming attraction. But they belonged to an affair, not to marriage. If ever a man seemed to have a positive allergy to commitment, it was Craig. Short-lived fun, that was all he would ever offer. Just the sort of relationship she most despised. He was still waiting for her reply. She frowned, trying to be honest.

'I don't object to marriage,' she told him. 'I'd even like to get married one day. It's just that I've seen so many broken bits of marriages around, and the fall-out from them, that I'd take a lot of convincing that my own could work. And I don't want to marry anyone I can't expect to stay married to.'

'Is that because of your mother?' he asked, his voice almost kind for once.

She was again surprised that he remembered what she had told him in Greece. But she didn't want to talk about her mother. She shrugged. 'Partly. Partly what's happened to some of my friends. Perhaps I just want to keep my belief in happy endings,' she mocked herself. He was too close to something that made her very uncomfortable, and she preferred their more usual sparring to this interest.

'I might have guessed you were a romantic at heart under that unconvincing air of common sense,' he teased.

'What do you mean?' It was obviously an insult, but at least it was a return to his familiar provocative style.

'For a start, no one with a shred of real common sense would be in your present situation.' Ruefully, she had to admit that was probably true. 'Secondly, only a romantic manages to retain such high-flown illusions about marriage, or anything else.' An almost bitter cynicism convinced her he wasn't just being his usual flippant self.

'So, disillusion me,' she challenged. She didn't want to believe what she was hearing, but at the same time she felt that in some ways she was discovering more about the real Craig Stanton than the charmer of Syntagma Square would ever have allowed.

He stared out at the passing cars before turning back to her. With his sudden honesty she had the feeling that their relationship had taken another step. Where to, she was uncomfortably uncertain.

'Sale and exchange. That's what life's ultimately about. If you're lucky, you get a good bargain.' She was chilled to the bone by the indifference in his voice, and the fathomless grey of his eyes was as remote as a distant moon. Perhaps he saw her distaste, because he focused on her and seemed willing to explain. 'All those romantic ideas, love in particular,' he said deliberately, 'are just other words for *want*. They're a sort of pretty cover for people's real, selfish desires. Emotional involvement's a sort of trap, trading on someone else's weakness, that's all.'

The brutal words hurt. She didn't want to believe he meant them, but they fitted too well with all he had said and done so far. He didn't even seem to realise how hard he sounded. She realised with grim and growing anger that, to him, they were just simple facts discovered the hard way. Not for the first time, she wished she had known the parents who had given him every worldly advantage and apparently no affection at all. It wasn't fair, Jane thought; no one should have to be that self-contained. He was leaning back in his seat, sunlight through the car window warming the hint of gold in his hair, his face impassive.

'So what's the point of helping me?' she challenged.

It didn't unsettle him. 'To trap the baddies, remember?' he said lightly. It wasn't the answer she'd hoped for, and she didn't think it was the whole truth—after all, he'd gone to some trouble to find her. She waited. A resigned look crossed his face. 'Besides, you came charging to *my* rescue in Athens.'

She believed him. Unfortunately. It all fitted too well. On his balance sheet he was in her debt again and he didn't like it. Sale and exchange, she remembered. There was nothing personal about this at all. Jane shivered, cold despite the sunshine.

'You don't owe me anything.' Somehow it was important to convince him. She might as well try to convince a stone.

'No? That's not what you said in Athens.' She remembered her impulsive accusation and demand for information, and regretted it bitterly. He shrugged. 'Anyway, we're almost at the shop, so you'd better start thinking what sort of ring you'd like.'

'"Like" isn't the operative word,' she reminded him tartly, following him out of the taxi, feeling increasingly depressed. Just how much more disastrous could the day become? she wondered gloomily, fearing that it was a long way from over yet.

'Look on it as a stage prop,' he suggested. 'You can give it back or sell it or something when this is all over if you don't want to keep it as a souvenir.'

Memories of the photography session in Athens were unavoidable, and unwelcome. 'I doubt if I'll need anything to help me remember,' she told him with unexpected heat.

He glanced sharply sideways at her, but only said, 'Here we are,' as he gestured towards a shop doorway.

Contrary to her expectations, they weren't outside a glossy Bond Street shop. The taxi had drawn up by a small building in a side-street she didn't recognise.

'We might find something in here,' he suggested.

The shop was dark and small, but the few pieces in the window were exquisite.

'You may be right,' Jane agreed, her reluctance increasing rapidly. Couldn't a chain-store jeweller have provided what they wanted? This was a mockery.

Inside, despite the gloomy lighting, gems glowed brilliantly. A small, balding man came hurrying forward when he saw them enter.

'Mr Craig!' he exclaimed. 'It's been too long, far too long! What can I do for you?'

So he didn't buy diamonds for all his girlfriends here. Craig was smiling, shaking the elderly man's hand with unusual warmth.

'Years ago, you made me promise to buy my future wife's engagement ring from you. So here I am.' He tugged Jane forward. She felt uncharacteristically diffident. It wasn't fair to involve this man's obvious affection for Craig in their sham of an engagement. She wanted to protest, but the firm clasp on her hand tightened warningly before he released it and turned to introduce her.

'Jane, this is Sam Isaacs, who's known me for longer than I'd like to admit. Sam, this is Jane Simpson.'

'I helped his father find a ring for his mother,' confided the old man. 'It was a lovely emerald,' he remembered with enthusiasm.

'So what are you offering the next generation?' Craig asked. Jane wondered if she was imagining his reluctance to discuss his parents.

The little jeweller was looking at her, hesitating. For an odd moment she thought he was seeing beyond the calm surface of her appearance to the doubts and turmoil beneath. Then he turned to a tray displayed under the glass of the counter.

'These are all engagement rings,' he said.

Most were diamonds, some bracketing other precious stones such as sapphires or rubies. They dazzled, but she could not imagine wearing any of them. They would do for the pretence, she supposed. Beside her, Craig frowned.

'They might impress the journalists when we make the announcement,' he decided, his words uncannily echoing her thoughts, 'but they're not really you. A bit too orthodox, I suspect,' he added with feeling.

'Would you mind something old-fashioned?' It was Sam's suggestion. Jane felt Craig's assessing glance on her.

'I've never thought of her as old-fashioned,' he said cautiously.

But Jane was looking at the tray Sam had taken from the safe. 'It's lovely!' she whispered, hardly daring to breathe.

There were half a dozen rings, all old, holding a variety of stones, but her hand had reached out almost involuntarily to pick up the big square-cut topaz bracketed by diamond chips in an intricate setting. Craig moved closer, looking down at the lovely ring.

'That's perfect.' For once there wasn't a hint of mockery. 'With those golden eyes of yours, it couldn't be better,' he observed, watching the ring, not her. 'Will it do?'

'I can't imagine anything better,' she admitted. It seemed almost wicked to use something so beautiful just as a sham, but she couldn't bear to wear any of the other glittery stones which were displayed.

Sam was smiling. 'A good choice; it's a stone of character, not something cold and hard. This one is unique and has a hint of mystery in it.'

Jane looked down at the stone, which seemed to have warmed in the heat of her palm. She heard Craig's voice say, with a hint of humour, 'I said it was perfect,' then he had lifted it from her hand, weighing it for a moment in his own before slipping it on to her ring finger. The fit was perfect. 'There. It's official now,' he told her.

She stared down at the yellow-gold glow on her left hand, feelings too complicated and confused for analysis disturbing her. It felt almost *too* right. 'I'm speechless,' she managed. Despite their conversation as they entered the shop, the symbolism of the gesture troubled her, as had the way Craig's hand had lingered for a moment on her own.

He was chuckling, and the moment of tension eased. 'That must be a first,' he said to Sam, who was beaming contentedly, evidently well pleased with their choice.

Back in the taxi, Jane was still unusually subdued. She couldn't get rid of the sense that something more important than the purchase of a theatrical prop had just happened. She stared at the ring, and then looked up at Craig, who was watching her, his expression ambiguous.

'It's not what I expected,' she said at last.

He smiled. 'It's not what I intended. But you have to admit that it suits you.' For once the teasing lacked malice.

'It's not going to be easy to give back,' she admitted.

'Since I can't imagine anyone else wearing it, that doesn't matter.' She was about to object when he went on, 'Anyway, since you've soothed my fevered brow, possibly saved me from pneumonia with your rug, and undoubtedly saved me from several severe bruises in Athens, you might say you've more than earned it already.'

Abruptly, she felt cold. All her pleasure in the ring evaporated. Of course. How could she have forgotten? He was in her debt. In his philosophy, that was an intolerable situation. He saw obligations as burdens, and Craig Stanton travelled light. He would pay her back in whatever currency he thought she would accept—his protection, the ring—as fast as he could. And then he would disappear. This was just a downpayment.

'What's wrong?'

She would have to guard against his quick perception of her moods. Theirs was an arrangement for her safety, that was all, and the sooner she let him discharge his imaginary debt and get out of her life, the better.

'Nothing.' She managed a slightly shaken laugh. 'I remember thinking in Greece that we'd had a fairly eventful first couple of meetings and wondering what the next would lead to. Even my imagination didn't come up with this,' she laughed ruefully, gesturing with her left hand.

His chuckle echoed her. 'Never mind. If Toby and his minions work well, it should only take a couple of weeks and then you can get back to whatever you're doing now. What *are* you doing, anyway?' he asked. 'I'd rather got used to the schoolmarm idea.'

'When I wasn't playing Florence Nightingale?' she reminded him. They were on the way to her flat to pick up some clothes; both Toby and Craig had flatly refused to let her go back there on her own, or to stay there for another night. She supposed there was no reason not to tell him, even if he did laugh at her. They would have to have something to talk about in the next few days, after all. 'I went into teaching because it seemed safe and stable and worthwhile,' she admitted, 'and that's what I thought I wanted.'

He was looking faintly stunned. 'I don't believe this is the same person who accosted a stranger at night on a Greek ferry and drove off three muggers almost single-handed. Where does safety come into all that?'

She chuckled, he seemed honestly bewildered. 'That's the trouble. I seem to have inherited characteristics from both my parents and, like them, they don't live together well. The teaching was fine at first,' she went on more seriously, 'but recently it's seemed to be stifling me. When Dad died last year I inherited some money, so I decided to see if I could make a career from writing—and be a bit more adventurous at the same time. Things seem to have got a little out of hand,' she acknowledged before he could comment.

'That's an understatement,' he agreed drily. 'What sort of writing?' Was he really interested? Probably not, but he had asked.

'Journalism: newspaper and magazine articles; what are vaguely called human interest stories. I had a couple of things accepted while I was still teaching, plus some encouraging noises from the people who'd bought them. I reckon I've enough money for a year in London, with care, to see whether I can make a living. What with one thing and another, though, I haven't written much lately,' she admitted, thinking of the unfinished article on Greek travel that she had promised to complete by the end of the week.

'I see. Well, you can always turn to fiction and write up our story,' he suggested lightly.

'Too improbable. I'm not sure I believe it myself. Look, we've arrived. You go and talk to Sally—you can even break the news if you like—while I go and pack a case suitable for all occasions.'

'You needn't bother with your ferry gear,' he told her as they went upstairs together.

She laughed. When had her mood changed? From gloom and depression she suddenly felt exhilarated, almost eager at the prospect of Craig and herself duping the public and their pursuers over the next few days. His reluctance to accept Toby's plans had made it clear enough that she needn't worry about any assault from him. As long as she ignored her own awareness of the chemistry between them, perhaps she could just enjoy the next few days. And at least she wouldn't have to sleep with the smell of paint for a while.

It didn't take long to fill a suitcase, pick up her typewriter, and return to Sally's door. Her friend greeted her with an impulsive hug. 'He's gorgeous,' she whispered in Jane's ear. 'You kept him pretty dark, didn't you?'

'Positively obscure.' Craig had clearly overheard at least the last part of the comment. 'It was fairly sudden for both of us, but we decided it was worth a try.'

Sally giggled and hugged Jane again. Then she reached up to brush a kiss against Craig's cheek and retreated into the flat, leaving them to make their way back down to the waiting taxi. Jane was quiet at first; it was absurd to be annoyed with Sally's funning, especially since Craig had enjoyed it, and she tried to shake off the unreasonable mood.

'Something wrong?' His voice broke into her thoughts and she hoped they hadn't been too apparent.

'No. Just trying to convince myself that this is really happening,' she told him. 'Did Toby issue orders for the rest of the day?' It was he who had suggested the ring.

'No. I think we play it by ear from now on. I'll phone a notice to the papers—including all the more gossipy rags—and then I'll have to leave you to your own devices for a while. I really do have an exhibition opening next week and not enough time to prepare for it. There's a mound of stuff still to process and mount. Why don't we go out and dazzle the town tonight, though? After all, Toby does want us to be conspicuous.' He presented the argument for an evening's revelry with deep serious-ness and she chuckled.

'I'm not sure I can dazzle anyone,' she warned, 'but orders are orders.'

He grinned. 'That's settled.'

The spare room he showed her to when they arrived at his house was on the floor above the living-room and decorated in soft shades of blue. It was light and airy and there was a desk beneath one window which would be ideal for working.

'This is fabulous,' she told him. 'If I'd known about the working conditions, I'd have signed on earlier.'

'Toby should have known that—it might have made his job easier. See you this evening. If there's anything you want, call me—I'm downstairs—or raid the kitchen.' He left before she could reply.

Was that to be the policy? Polite attention to the guest and a little humour when the situation warranted? It should at least make it easier to ignore that tug of attraction she couldn't help but feel whenever they were together, and he at least seemed to be untroubled by the chemistry. She'd be quite safe; she could just look on the whole thing as an adventure. It was ridiculous to feel slightly let down by his apparent preference for work over her company. With some irritation, she began to unpack.

To her own surprise, the afternoon passed quickly. She even managed to type up some of the notes she had brought with her. She did go down once to make some tea, but saw no sign of Craig and did not feel the need to seek him out.

Later that evening, she surveyed her wardrobe, wondering how to 'dazzle the town'. There wasn't a great deal of choice, but black always suited her. The dress was deceptively plain, until she had it on. A simple silk camisole top met an intricately pleated skirt below a dropped waist, falling to a handkerchief-pointed hem which swirled around her slim legs. The curves she deplored were alluringly feminine under the softly draped fabric. The plain gold necklace and earrings which were the best her jewellery-case afforded offset the silk perfectly, leaving the topaz to glow dramatically on her left hand, making her slender fingers seem almost fragile. She slipped her feet into high-heeled black sandals and turned away from the mirror.

Hesitantly, half excited, half intimidated at the thought of the evening to come, she went down to the first-floor living-room. He was already there, sleek and formal and remote in his evening dress, the hair for once disciplined, the grey eyes opaque and untrustworthy. He looked at her without expression as she entered, and she was suddenly nervous. Then he lifted the glass from the table by his side and raised it in a toast, his quick smile lop-sided and teasing.

'You know,' he told her lightly, 'if you go on looking like that, no one is going to be in the least surprised at our betrothal. In fact, I rather think I'm going to have to fight off some competition.' If anything, he looked pleased at the prospect. 'Shall we go?'

It was an enchanted evening. They dined at an intimate French restaurant where the waiters seemed to know Craig and, although a few people looked up from their seats to greet him, no one intruded on their privacy.

From time to time as they dined Jane was aware of Craig's eyes lingering on her face, a softer smile than the one she was used to lifting a corner of his expressive mouth. Beneath the poise created by confidence in her own appearance, bolstered by the warm approval she had seen in his eyes earlier, her own resolve to treat the situation just as an adventure was crumbling. For the moment at least, Craig seemed to have abandoned his habitual barbed irony.

The fingers of one hand toyed with the long stem of his wine glass as, with the other, he absently brushed back the lock of hair that had fallen over his forehead. Her hands longed to smooth it back.

'Enjoying yourself?' he wondered lazily, his glance dwelling with apparent approval on her.

'Immensely.' It was true. 'This is a rare treat for me—dining out lately has tended to be the Indian take-away on the corner or the Italian trattoria across the road,' she told him. 'They're both good value, but they lack the style of this place.' Her gesture indicated the quiet elegance of the décor and the attentive but unobtrusive service.

'The surroundings suit you.' He seemed mildly surprised by his own quick compliment, but showed no signs of retracting or qualifying it.

Not his usual style at all, Jane thought, pleased as she realised there was no underlying irony. The heavy ring on her left hand caught her eye and she twisted it, still enchanted by its beauty as well as amazed to be wearing it.

He noticed the action. 'How's your mother going to take the news?' he wondered.

She grimaced. 'I suppose I will have to tell her. If I don't, someone else is sure to.' He chuckled at the gloom in her voice. She explained, 'I'm afraid she'll be delighted, even though she does seem rather preoccupied with the merits of rich Texans these days.'

His smile was sympathetic as he considered the matter. 'You could always point out that you've found your own rich Englishman,' he suggested. She must have shown her momentary incomprehension. 'Me. Contrary to first impressions,' he added.

It hadn't really occurred to her. She'd known he had money, of course—the Athens hotel had told her that—but she hadn't consciously thought of him as wealthy. She thought of the Chelsea house. It wasn't ostentatious but the antiques, the richly patterned rugs, the general air of lived-in elegance, should have told her. It just wasn't something she usually thought about.

'She'll be even more furious when I tell her it's all over,' she decided ruefully, trying to ignore the odd pain that she felt at the thought.

'We needn't rush to end it, need we?' he asked plaintively. 'After all, we only became engaged this morning.'

And how. 'Don't forget Athens,' she reminded him.

'How could I?' Perhaps it hadn't been a good idea to recall that day. She looked down at her plate, fiddling with a spoon, then pushing it aside.

How did she really feel about this masquerade? It was lunacy, and it was as safe as lighting a fire in a munitions factory, but, having been more or less forced into it, she couldn't honestly say she was regretting it. Not yet.

Craig must have been following his own train of thoughts. 'Haven't you ever wanted to go and live in America?' he wondered.

Had she? She had thought of it once, but rejected the idea. Her father had still been alive and it would have seemed like abandoning him. She shrugged. 'When Mum finally got round to marrying Ben, we'd rather lost touch, and all my friends were here.' She glanced up at him, her own smile slightly uneven. 'I wasn't really convinced the marriage would last—her track-record's not very good.' Now, she thought it might last, but then remembered how the marriage to her father had fallen apart after eleven years.

He raised an eyebrow, leaning back in his chair. 'For a newly engaged couple, we seem to be unusually sceptical about the endurance capacity of marriage.'

'At least that gives us something in common,' she pointed out drily.

'True. I wonder what else we'll discover in the next few days?' he speculated. Abruptly her assumption that he would ignore the chemistry was shaken. Her hand was not quite steady as she carefully put down her napkin. Fortunately she was spared the need to reply by the approach of a familiar figure. Craig looked up as he stopped by their table, and groaned.

'I might have known it. You can't beat the Civil Service for nosiness.' He didn't sound particularly annoyed as he turned to the man, who was smiling amiably. 'Hello,

Toby. I suppose we shouldn't be surprised to see you here?'

'Of course not. I'm delighted to see you both again, especially you, Miss Simpson,' he said heartily and turned back to Craig. 'You ought to be thanking me, my boy, not reviling my department and all its works,' he told him bluntly. 'I'm beginning to think we've done you a very good turn indeed.'

Perhaps she should have been sobered by this reminder of the real reason she and Craig were together, but it was difficult to take Toby seriously and, besides, she enjoyed hearing Craig described as 'my boy'. He must have been used to it because he only smiled derisively. 'Santa Claus lives?' he suggested.

'Why not?' Toby demanded, sounding half serious. 'Now I'll leave you to celebrate on your own—but you don't intend keeping her entirely to yourself, I hope?' Was that a hint?

Craig looked at Jane, his clear eyes holding hers for a long moment. 'It's beginning to seem like a very appealing idea,' he said slowly. Then, before she could register either alarm or protest, or even the sudden surge of pleasure that his words gave her, he grinned. 'But tonight I intend to show her off and bask in general congratulations. Next stop's the nearest nightclub.'

'Good idea. Enjoy yourselves,' the older man approved, smiling benevolently on them both before wandering off, deceptively aimless.

'You heard our orders,' said Craig. 'Shall we go?'

He took her arm and led her out through the well-bred hush of the restaurant. Jane had the feeling that a quiet murmur of gossip was waiting to break out behind them. The thought wasn't entirely displeasing.

The atmosphere of 'the nearest nightclub'—which turned out to be exclusive and expensive and a short taxi-ride away—was altogether different. Some names and faces she recognised, others were unfamiliar; all of them watched her with increased interest and speculation when they heard of the engagement. Glances lingered appraisingly on the lovely topaz. For the first time in her life, Jane felt confident and assured in such a gathering as she walked to their table with her arm tucked into Craig's.

At the table, he ordered champagne and they lifted their glasses in conspiratorial salute. No one was going to be able to accuse him of hiding his fiancée away. Other friends and acquaintances stopped by to shout words of congratulations to him; twice, flashbulbs exploded near them and she caught his grin.

'Makes a change to be on the other side of the lens,' he told her cheerfully. 'Shall we dance?'

Well, no one came here for light conversation. She got to her feet and took the hand he held out to her.

The tiny dance-floor was too crowded for energetic displays. At first they danced apart but near to each other, finding no difficulty in matching each other's steps. When, inevitably, the beat slackened and became more intimate, Craig reached out to draw her towards him.

Under the pulsing lights that intermittently lit the floor, Jane saw the smile that creased his thin face. He knew exactly what she was thinking, she realised. This might be a very public statement of their relationship, but it was also very thin ice indeed, and he was reminding her of the element in their relationship which she was determined to ignore. Trying to subdue her own awareness and instant reaction to his nearness and his hands on her, she matched his expression with her own defiant grin and felt, as much as heard, his responsive chuckle. Amusement, as much as their public surroundings, defused the situation. She clasped her hands lightly round his neck, allowing herself to enjoy the luxury of touching him in relative safety, and relaxed to the gentle rhythm of the music, her body moving instinctively in tune with his.

When the music's tempo changed again, they walked in silence back to their table. She wondered if he was as reluctant as she to shatter the fragile harmony which the dance had spun between them.

He sat beside, not opposite her and she was conscious of his closeness as he turned to pour champagne into the long, fluted glasses.

'To an interesting engagement?' he suggested, lifting his glass.

She hesitated. It was a toast which offered too many possibilities. 'Shouldn't the key word be "safe"?' she wondered.

Even in the noisy room, she was aware of his soft chuckle. 'Definitely not. You haven't been noticeably associated with safety in any of our encounters so far, and I should hate to see things change now. You might be infuriating, but at least you're never likely to be dull.' There was conviction behind the laughter.

It was a back-handed sort of compliment, if it was one. But he had a point—and her common-sense side took another step backwards. 'I can't—I *daren't*—guarantee to maintain my remarkable record, but I agree: here's to interesting times.' She touched her glass gently against his, excitement that had nothing at all to do with champagne bubbling in her veins. He watched her as she drank, a smile creasing his cheek and the expression in his eyes almost questioning as he raised his own glass to his lips. The moment stretched out between them.

'The ancient Chinese used that toast as a curse, you know.' A clear female voice broke the spell.

Jane looked up. A tall, elegant women, jet-black hair swept into a complicated and sleek knot, jade-green dress shimmering with beads, stood beside their table.

'Hello,' said Craig without enthusiasm, and without getting up. 'Have you come to congratulate us?'

'No. Only to hope your wishes come true. For both you and your fiancée,' she snapped, poison dripping from the last two words. Then she turned, sharp heels digging into the polished floor, and walked quickly away.

'Now, that,' commented Jane carefully, unsure what it had all been about but beginning for the first time that evening to feel out of her depth, 'was what I meant by "tall, elegant and sophisticated".'

'And expensive,' Craig reminded her. 'And in a filthy temper,' he added unnecessarily. 'She didn't stay long enough to be introduced. Her name's Jillian Shaw.'

'I see.' She did. Craig looked a question and she explained drily, 'Toby mentioned her at lunchtime. Remember?'

'Ah, yes.' He didn't sound in the least disconcerted and his glance, unlike Jane's, had not even followed the woman as she had stalked back to her own table. 'Well, you can always protect me from *her* if you feel the need,' he murmured.

On the dance-floor the lights dimmed and the music slowed again. Craig looked at Jane and, without hesitation, she stood up, moving naturally into his arms. For this evening, at least, he seemed to value her unpredictability above the more evident and enduring charms of a woman like Jillian. Since it couldn't last, and wouldn't go any further, she might as well make the most of it. But when she caught a glimpse over Craig's shoulder of the other woman she couldn't help but see the jealousy and distress on the lovely face and the slight surge of triumph died away. She never wanted to suffer like that over anyone. She turned her head into the dark fabric of Craig's jacket and felt his hold tighten slightly on her waist.

Hours later, on the way back to Chelsea in the early hours of the morning, she felt distinctly pleased with the evening. It had certainly had its moments. The desired public impression had been made but, more than that, she had enjoyed both being with Craig and the faint exhilaration of pretending to ignore the current of attraction which ran silently between them. The next few days might, after all, be manageable as well as interesting. It also occurred to her that not once during the evening had she felt that uncomfortable sense of being followed. Fleetingly, she wondered whether this charade would turn out after all to be an unnecessary exercise.

'Coffee?' Craig offered as they went upstairs.

She wasn't at all tired. 'Lovely,' she agreed, and wandered into the living-room, kicking off her high-heeled sandals and tucking her feet beneath her on the ample sofa.

When he came back from the kitchen he had taken off the formal jacket and opened the neck of his white dress shirt. 'Here,' he said, offering a mug to her.

'Thanks.' She took it, cupping it in both hands, suddenly glad of something to focus on, because he hadn't taken the nearby armchair. He was sitting at the far end of the sofa, turned sideways to lean against its arm, watching her. She could feel his eyes on her, trying to read her thoughts, and she didn't want to look at him in case he saw her sudden uncertainty.

'It was a good evening,' she said lamely. Anything, however banal, was better than awkward silence.

'Very.' He didn't seem to be feeling any awkwardness at all. In fact he was wholly at ease. She sensed rather than saw him put down his own drink. 'I've been wondering——' he began.

'What?' she asked incautiously.

He reached out, taking the mug from her and setting it aside before touching her face, turning her so that she had to look at him.

'Whether what happened in Athens was as remarkable as I remember,' he told her quietly.

FOUR
IRRESISTIBLE
TEMPTATIONS
FREE!
☆☆ **PLUS** ☆☆

Temptations offer you all the age-old joy and tenderness of romance, now experienced through very contemporary relationships...

And to introduce to you this powerful and highly charged series, we'll send you *four Temptation romances* absolutely **FREE** when you complete and return this card.

We're so confident that you'll enjoy Temptations that we'll also reserve a subscription for you, to our Reader Service, which means that you'll enjoy...

- **FOUR BRAND NEW NOVELS** – sent direct to you each month (before they're available in the shops).

- **FREE POSTAGE AND PACKING** – we pay all the extras.

- **FREE REGULAR NEWSLETTER** – packed with special offers, competitions, author news and much more...

This lovely Teddy Bear measures just 7 inches. His brown eyes and adorable expression make him the perfect cuddly companion!

☆☆ **PLUS** ☆☆

A
MYSTERY
GIFT

>>>> **CLAIM THESE GIFTS OVERLEAF** >>>>

FREE BOOKS CERTIFICATE

YES! Please send me **four FREE Temptations** together with my **FREE gifts.** Please also reserve a special Reader Service subscription for me. If I decide to subscribe, I will receive four Temptation romances each month for just £6.60 postage and packing free. If I decide not to subscribe I shall write to you within 10 days. The free books and gifts are mine to keep in any case. I understand that **I am under no obligation whatsoever.**

I may cancel or suspend my subscription at any time simply by writing to you. I am over 18 years of age.

7AIT

NAME _____

ADDRESS _____

_____ POSTCODE _____

SIGNATURE _____

FREE GIFT

Return this card now and we'll also send you this cuddly Teddy Bear absolutely FREE together with...

MYSTERY GIFT

We all
love
mysteries,
so as well
as the
FREE
Teddy
Bear
there's an
intriguing
FREE gift specially for you.

POST TODAY!

MILLS & BOON
FREEPOST
P.O. BOX 236
CROYDON
CR9 9EL

mps

CHAPTER SIX

SHE should have been backing away, rejecting the purpose she saw in the grey eyes and sensuous mouth before he acted. He was giving her time. She felt the blood mount in her cheeks and her pulse begin to race under the touch of his fingers. Her lips parted involuntarily as warmth flooded her body. He cupped her face between his palms; they seemed cool to her heated skin. For a long moment he held her like that and she watched, puzzled and breathless, trying to read the emotions in the fine-drawn face. Behind the amusement and curiosity, the flare of kindling passion, she thought for a second that she glimpsed an odd hesitation. Ridiculous. There was nothing at all hesitant in the lips which touched hers.

It was her last coherent thought for several minutes. His lips coaxed hers apart, his tongue seeking and teasing her own. One hand slid into her hair, holding her head, while the other traced the line of her neck, skimming the curves of her body before settling at her waist to draw her towards him.

There was never, there never could be, any question of being his unwilling partner, or even of remaining passive in his embrace. The urgent fire that had flared between them once before had them both in its grip; her arms were around his neck, urging him closer. The wide, soft cushions of the sofa were beneath them now and her body lay half under the strength of his.

When his lips left hers she murmured something, nothing, at being deprived of their caress. But then she gasped as she felt their delicate touch tracing the column of her neck, her shoulders, bringing each place he touched to urgent and unfamiliar life. Gentle hands brushed aside the narrow black straps of her dress, lips lingering in their place.

The tide of passion rose to engulf her but, despite the clamour of her body's response to his seeking lips, she knew a last moment of clarity. Hours ago, when Toby had pushed them into the engagement, she had known this would happen. Unconsciously, she might even have sought it as eagerly as his hands now sought the swell of her breasts. But she wasn't ready, not yet.

It was all happening too fast. In a moment she would be drowning in the surge of pleasure that was sweeping her along. Desire was burning too high, too fiercely. And desire was not, never would be, enough. She braced her hands against his shoulders, willing herself to push him away, maddeningly conscious of the hard warmth of his muscled flesh beneath the soft cotton of his shirt, his weight against her breasts. Hands that had meant to reject began to caress. Again she caught herself. Memories of jealous, hurt eyes across a dance-floor, of the idiotic, giggling girls in Athens, lent her resolve. This time she moved herself away from him, away from the promise of his questing hands. The back of the sofa prevented real retreat, but he read her intention and looked up, one hand reaching to brush aside the curls which clung to her forehead.

'No?' he queried, a hint of laughter in his voice.

Take it lightly, she told herself. 'No,' she agreed, wishing her voice carried more conviction.

He lay beside her a moment longer, the slight pressure of his legs against hers a reminder of her vulnerability. She wasn't at all sure she could find the will-power to repeat that refusal if he chose to test it. Then he swung his legs to the floor, running long, thin fingers through his already tousled hair before getting up in one easy movement. He glanced down at her and the explicit look in the grey eyes had her hastily restoring order to her dress and retreating to the far end of the sofa.

He stooped to pick up their drinks. 'Coffee's cold,' he noticed. 'I'll make some more.'

His coolness and capacity for making her self-conscious while so quickly regaining his own balance was infuriating. Suddenly she was angry, wanting to blame him for that collapse of self-control which had left her helpless and which had apparently left him undisturbed. She couldn't run away. She was trapped here for several days at least—she didn't like to think how long—and attack was her only defence of a resistance that was paper thin. And whose flimsiness he probably knew.

'Is the tumble on the sofa in lieu of rent?' she asked quietly, hating the edge in her voice, regretting the nasty comment almost before it was spoken.

At least it got a reaction. 'No!' His voice was even after that first protest, but there was real anger in it. 'You don't owe me anything. If you can't accept that this...' he gestured impatiently at the rumpled cushions, her dishevelled clothes '...is something we both want, then that's an end of it.' She shrank from the hostility in his voice, but then he laughed, not quite steadily, and was her familiar antagonist again. His shrug was almost rueful. 'Just don't expect me to give up trying to persuade you otherwise,' he warned her lightly as he walked towards the kitchen.

Round two to Craig, she decided. He had definitely emerged less battered than she from that particular squabble. She would hesitate before engaging him again. It made it no easier to know that he would not scruple to use his most powerful weapon, that almost tangible physical appeal, against her. Why on earth had she ever thought he would ignore it? Oh, he wouldn't force her; he would even let her say no. The trouble was that he evidently didn't expect her to keep on saying no. A reluctant smile tugged at her lips. She didn't indulge in casual affairs, but this was such new territory for her that, in the end, it might be her determination to defeat his assurance which provided her best protection.

'What are you smiling at?' His voice broke her thoughts and he put a steaming cup beside her.

There was an early chill to the air and she was grateful for the warmth of the drink. Still smiling slightly, but deciding it was more prudent not to reveal her thoughts, she shook her head. 'Nothing.'

He might not have believed her, but he made no comment. She heard quiet footsteps on the carpet behind her and then a drift of soft fabric settled on her bare shoulders.

'Since you won't let me keep you warm in any other way and I'd hate you to catch a cold on your first night in my house, you'd better wear this.'

She touched the lovely fabric, a rich Paisley of greens and golds in a wool so fine that it hung like silk against her. 'It's beautiful!' she exclaimed. She had no intention of commenting on what else he had said, nor of looking at him.

'I picked it up in Camden Lock the other day,' he explained. 'Not, you understand, that I often wear shawls myself, but I tend to hoard such things if they take my fancy. They often come in handy as accessories if I do any studio work downstairs.'

'So you do portraits?' she asked, grateful for the change of subject and conscious of how little she really knew of him or his work.

He grimaced. 'Some. I did more when I was trying to get established, but it's really a dead end. You tend to be written off as a society or fashion photographer, and nothing else. Your name may become well known, but you're not taken very seriously. When I realised that, I shut the studio and went walkabout for a year.'

'Where?' she wondered, intrigued. Here, at least, was something that did matter to him.

'Started in the States, then teamed up with some college graduates who wanted to ''do'' India and Afghanistan by foot and truck.' He smiled reminiscently. 'It had its moments, but I managed to survive with only minor dysentery and a rat bite.'

'And a book of photographs?' she deduced.

'That's it. Yes, I was lucky. It was fairly successful and people began to show more interest in my work. From time to time I was given a chance at other exotic locations.'

'Like the Middle East?' she asked drily.

'Not always quite that dramatic.' He smiled. 'But it's far more interesting than society portraits, even with the occasional little local difficulty thrown in,' he said cheerfully. 'Now I only take the faces that interest me, and I don't much care if I find them in Regent's Park or Timbuctoo. Or Athens,' he added deliberately.

Her snort of laughter was expressively dismissive of that session in Syntagma Square.

'Especially Athens,' he insisted firmly. 'And, by the way, I was right.'

'Inevitably.' She yawned and added, unwisely, 'About what?'

'Us. It was every bit as remarkable as I remembered.'

She couldn't flounce out and go home. Nor was it exactly the moment to tell him she was going to bed. His response would be too predictable. Anyway, he was right: there was no point in lying, even to herself, about that incendiary reaction. Instead she managed to meet the faint challenge in the amused grey eyes with a half-smile of her own, hoping he could not detect the tension which tightened her clasp on the cooling mug, the see-saw of doubt and indecision which was confusing her.

'Yes,' she agreed quietly. 'And my reply remains the same.'

'Put the chemistry set back in the cupboard?' he remembered.

'And lock it away,' she confirmed. And throw away the key, she added to herself.

'It must be your stubbornness I find so appealing. You just don't know how to give in, do you?' Don't I?

she thought ruefully, but said nothing. 'It *is* going to be an interesting engagement,' he added with evident anticipation.

'It sounds more like the curse that your friend Jillian threatened us with,' she told him gloomily.

He grinned. 'We'll see. But perhaps we'd better defer the next instalment for a while. It's been quite a day and you're beginning to look as though you need some sleep. I'd hate to take an unfair advantage.'

In a pig's ear, she thought uncharitably, but had enough sense to keep the thought to herself. She suppressed another huge yawn. 'I *am* tired,' she agreed reluctantly.

How did he manage both to provoke and defuse such a powerfully charged situation in a matter of minutes? It was exasperating, but if this was a reprieve she was going to take it.

Jane stretched lazily in the wide bed next morning after a surprisingly untroubled night's sleep. Rain was tapping lightly against the window and the bed was warm and soft. Reluctantly, she opened her eyes. Something, and it hadn't been an alarm clock, had woken her. A soft tap, more positive than the gentle sound of the rain, was repeated, followed this time by the sound of the door opening.

'Room service,' said a cheerful voice.

She turned over slowly, feeling distinctly at a disadvantage. She was glad that the pale yellow nightdress she was wearing was so unrevealing. If Craig was disappointed by its Victorian primness, he didn't show it.

'You look like a duckling,' he observed. 'Fluffy and rather endearing. The sort of creature that wants to be picked up and stroked?' It was half a question. She was fairly certain he was only teasing. Fairly.

She ran her fingers through the blonde curls, well aware of how chaotic they were first thing in the morning. 'Ducklings can deliver quite a nasty peck,' she warned him. Then she saw that he was carrying a tray. 'Is that tea?' she asked with more enthusiasm.

'It is. He put the tray down on the bedside table. 'Don't get too used to the service, though; it's just my devious way of telling you that I have to lock myself away downstairs for a few hours. Treat the house as your own—food in the fridge, and so on. The garden's usually quite nice, but I don't recommend it today.' He indicated the moisture sliding down the window-pane. 'And don't go domestic on me—someone comes in to do all the cleaning. If you want to ring round your friends to break the news, there's a phone in the living-room or you can swipe the extension from my room. There's a socket in here, by the desk.' He hesitated. 'Are you going to phone your mother?'

She grimaced. 'I can always write.'

'Coward. Use the phone and get it over with as soon as it's a civilised time of day in Texas. I'll see you later. You might enjoy the comments in some of the more vulgar papers,' he added as he turned to leave, indicating the small heap beside the cup on the tray.

He had strolled out before she could thank him.

The tea was welcome and, blast him, he was right: she ought to make some phone calls. Anyone who had been trying to contact her at the flat would begin to worry before long even if they didn't read the papers. She'd better look at them herself first.

The notices in most of them were conventional and predictable. There was a brief comment on a couple of the arts pages, usually in with some discussion of the forthcoming show, but she found one tabloid whose gossip columnist had clearly decided to go to town. There was a picture of Craig and one—had he supplied it?— of her that might have come from one of the Athens photographs. Fortunately it was too grainy to be a good likeness. It was the nauseatingly coy paragraph attached which made her wince. 'Speculation about Craig Stanton's latest companion ended today when he told

me, "Her name's Jane Simpson and we met in Greece."
Readers will be as astonished as your columnist was to
hear that, for this far-from-plain Jane, Craig intends to
abandon his cherished bachelor status. "We haven't set
a date for the wedding yet," he told me. "The engagement's still very new." All those other love-lorn ladies,
eat your hearts out. This column will keep you informed
about the season's most intriguing match yet.'

If other readers were astonished, Jane was appalled.
Then the humour of it struck her and she wished she
could have been there when Craig had phoned the writer.
Had he really managed to sound quite so cloying? She
chuckled, and tossed it to one side as she got up.

She dressed casually in jeans and a blue shirt, adding
a large multi-coloured knitted jacket because there was
a touch of coolness in the air. It was time to get the
phone calls done—and hope that few of her friends read
that ghastly tabloid. She decided to take him up on the
offer of his bedroom phone.

On the walls of the short corridor leading to his room
were three photographs. He'd said he kept his own work
up here, hadn't he? She hadn't looked at them yesterday
but now, knowing he was unlikely to appear, she stopped
to examine them. She realised afresh that this was in
some ways the 'real' Craig Stanton. They had none of
the dilettante disguise of so much of his conversation,
but that did not make them comfortable to be with. Two
were landscapes, both of them bleak and wild although
she suspected that the one of the open downland had
been taken not many miles from London, even if the
one of the desert was from somewhere altogether more
remote. She looked at the third picture. A girl was
walking away down an empty street. In some ways it was
even bleaker than the other two. Jane wondered what
mood he had been in when he had taken it. It looked
personal, somehow, and she felt as though she was
intruding.

Should she use the living-room phone after all? No. Hadn't he suggested she borrow the one from his room? If she was curious that was her business; she wasn't uninvited.

It was still with an uneasy sense of prying, however, that she turned the handle of the door at the end of the passage. She had even, foolishly, knocked first even though she knew he was two floors below.

The room was about the same size as the one she was using, but any similarity ended there. Hers was decorated in shades of blue, pictures hung on the walls and the bedspread was a bright patchwork of living colours. It was a room to relax in, designed to cosset and please its inhabitant. And she would have sworn the décor was Craig's own choice. His own taste, it seemed, was different. The room was almost monastic in its starkness. There was little furniture, except the wide double bed, its cover a heavy white cotton fabric in some intricate peasant weave, a military chest beside it and a table in a rich dark wood against a wall. Apart from an upright chair and the plain white doors of the built-in wardrobes, there was nothing. No pictures, no ornaments, no casual clutter. It was as though the room's owner had made a deliberate effort to leave no imprint on this most personal of rooms. She couldn't imagine him sharing it with a woman.

Jane shivered. Was this yet another aspect of Craig? If so, what did it imply? Restraint? Lack of character? The latter was inconceivable and the former implied a degree of self-control and discipline that she found alarming. Was he unwilling to reveal *any* personal feeling? Even on his own? There wasn't a single photograph to be seen.

She thought about the opulent informality of the living-room. That, she was convinced, was also a product of his own taste, not some designer's choice. The contrast with this bareness only deepened the enigma.

She had, she realised, naïvely assumed she would somehow, eventually, penetrate the façade she was well aware that he cultivated. Now she had her doubts. Feeling uncharacteristically subdued, she picked up the ivory-coloured handset from beside the bed and retreated to the comfort of her own room.

By the time she'd had a long chat with Sally and spoken briefly to the editor who was interested in her current work, confirming that it was almost ready, it was still much too early to phone Texas. Fortunately. Sally's repeated congratulations and questions had made her uncomfortable—she didn't like the way this deception was spreading to include so much of her life. Too many people were involved. It didn't help, either, that last night had confirmed her fears; she was trapped in an impossible situation. The attraction to Craig was as bad—if that was the right word—as it had ever been and he was still the sort of man who would commit himself to no one. She no longer even knew what she wanted, all she knew was what she risked by staying here with him. She did not like to contemplate what a short-lived affair, which was all he would offer, would do to her. The vague threat from the Athens thug seemed almost harmless in comparison.

The ring lying on the dressing-table caught her eye. She had hesitated to put it on this morning but, after only half a day of wearing it, her hand felt oddly weightless without it. She picked it up, and slipped it on to her finger. She paced the room, then stood by the window staring down at the wet street. The drizzle seemed to have stopped, but the day looked cold and dismal. Unappealing. At least it *should* have been unappealing. Unfortunately, knowing that she was confined to the house, she wanted to go out.

Unreasonably, and inevitably, she blamed Craig. It was his fault that she was trapped in his house. He could entertain her. She forgot that she had resolved not to impose on him, but hesitated for a moment longer. His

visit with the tray had contained a definite hint that he
didn't want to be disturbed. Then her eye was caught
by the Paisley shawl which she had folded over the arm
of a chair. Even in the gloom of a wet day, its colour
glowed jewel-bright.

She picked it up, unconsciously caressing its soft
texture. She would return his photographic prop to him.

Down two flights of stairs, Jane found herself facing
the front door. On her left was the shut, blank door to
the room in which she assumed Craig was working. She
looked at the door on to the street for a long moment.
She could never afterwards decide why she didn't simply
open it and go out alone for the walk she wanted.
Cowardice? Prudence? A promise to Craig? Or possibly
the feeling that it would be an easier option than interrupting his work, and where he was concerned she had
given up taking the easy option? Or did she just want
to see him again? She ignored that idea.

Resolutely, she turned away from the outer door and
towards the other one, knocking twice and turning the
handle before she could have second thoughts.

It was deflating to discover the room empty. She
looked around. The walls were stark white, the windows
screened by dark blinds. A tangle of complex wiring
snaked across the floor to a bewildering array of lights,
while movable screens in a range of colours and sizes
broke up the room's severe proportions. Incongruously,
there were odd items scattered around—hung on hooks
or draped over chair-backs: hats, a man's black umbrella,
a scattering of artificial flowers, an empty tankard. Was
that a prop, or lunch? Anyway, this was clearly where
the shawl belonged. She could just dump it, but that
seemed pointless.

'Who on earth's there?' The irritated voice came from
behind a door in the far wall. Above it, a red light
glowed: the dark-room

'Jane,' she called back. It sounded as though it *had*
been a mistake to come in here. Perversely, she felt her

confidence return. An angry Craig was someone she was used to. 'I've brought your shawl back,' she added helpfully.

There was silence for a long minute, then the red light clicked off and the door opened. He was wearing faded jeans and looked untidy, as though he had been running his hands through his hair again; the white shirt he wore was old and stained with the marks of ink or acid or something. Not for the first time, she wished she could control that instant reaction to him: the quickened pulse and heightened awareness. He scowled at her, wiping his hands on a rag. 'I told you, I don't wear shawls.'

'You said your models did.'

'Put it on, then.' The scowl had gone and there was the beginning of a softening to the severe line of his mouth, but his gaze was focusing on her with a sort of assessing detachment which she found disconcerting. The knitted jacket was suddenly scant protection and all her consciousness of her own physical limitations flared up.

'I'm not your model,' she pointed out tartly. She put the shawl on a chair and stepped away from it.

'You could be,' he said, his voice cool. 'You move well, and you've got an interesting face; it's very expressive.' He was watching her as though she were some object, not an individual, and she didn't like it. She was already too vulnerable to those probing eyes. She had seen his photography and she did not like to think what his camera might reveal about her.

'Yes. Well, at the moment what it should be expressing to someone as eagle-eyed as yourself is boredom. I'm going for a walk.' She hoped she didn't sound defiant.

He sighed. 'Posing for me would solve the boredom problem, but I suppose you won't accept that simple solution?'

'No. See you later.' She turned away, waiting for his reaction.

'Has it stopped raining?' He sounded resigned rather than angry.

'Yes. Why?'

'Because I don't enjoy walking in the rain. Go and get your coat.'

She turned back quickly. 'I don't need an escort,' she protested.

'Yes, you do. That's why we're engaged. Remember? Now, go and get your coat.' Impatience put an edge to his voice.

She realised she was behaving foolishly. 'Won't that just offer a double target?' she wondered.

'Probably. Do you still want a walk?'

She looked around the shuttered room. Outside was daylight, however gloomy; in here, time of day seemed irrelevant. 'Yes,' she said, suddenly emphatic.

His air of suppressed irritation vanished. 'It's a *very* expressive face,' he told her, grinning. 'You look half suffocated.'

'Thanks.' It was hardly a flattering image. 'You're right, of course,' she admitted.

'Come on, then.'

She ran back upstairs and found her old trenchcoat. When she returned he had on the familiar leather jacket and had retrieved the umbrella from among the props.

'Just in case,' he told her. He also had a camera bag over one shoulder, but made no comment on it.

The streets were damp and almost empty. An occasional car hissed past them on the wet tarmac, but there was little else to disturb the late morning peace.

They reached the entrance to a small park and he unlatched the gate for her. 'This time you can scuffle in damp leaves, but I don't advise paddling in the pond unless you want rheumatism.'

'Stop worrying about my health and treating me like a child,' she told him, aware that she had been behaving childishly. 'You're the one who's been less than healthy whenever we've met,' she reminded him.

His smile was reminiscent. 'How could I ever forget? And,' he added, no longer smiling, 'don't ever make the mistake of thinking I take you for a child.'

He was delving in his camera bag, his hands deft on the assortment of lenses. He didn't react to the long silence which followed that comment. She felt breathless, reminded of danger at a moment when she'd felt quite secure.

'What are you up to?' she demanded at last as he lifted the camera.

'Taking pictures. It's my job,' he added with transparently false patience. 'You don't have to pose, and if you end up in the shot it's my fault not yours.'

He was focusing on something else as he spoke. Was she being an idiot, after all, to be so self-conscious. It was a form of vanity, wasn't it? As he said, any pictures he took of her were his concern. As long as she was allowed to see them before they became public property. As for his other remarks, she would just have to take care not to offer him the openings he did not scruple to take. In a war of words, or of the senses, she had enough sense left to know when she was outclassed.

A fine drizzle began to drift down and she turned up her coat collar, laughing at Craig's attempts to manipulate both umbrella and camera before going over to relieve him of the former. He grinned his thanks and pointed the camera at her. Laughing, she ducked behind the black screen of the umbrella. If they could stay this relaxed with each other, perhaps the next few days wouldn't be so bad after all.

CHAPTER SEVEN

IT WAS probably inevitable that the camaraderie of that day could not last. Over the next week Craig was increasingly preoccupied with preparations for his exhibition, and Jane's feeling of being trapped only increased. Sally came round sometimes, but her unreserved enthusiasm for Craig, and her eagerness to talk about him, did little to make life easier. Nor did the promise he had extracted from her not to go out alone except in a taxi ordered and approved by Toby. It might be sensible, but it was rapidly becoming worse than being at boarding school. As a pupil.

Craig did maintain the role of the devoted fiancé in public, taking her out almost every evening to parties, or shows, or dinner. On the surface it might seem an enviable existence, Sally certainly thought it was, but the combination of tension and claustrophobia was beginning to wear Jane's nerves thin. She sometimes wondered whether Toby was doing anything at all, or whether there was anything to be done. Perhaps the letter had just been a bizarre threat designed only to put them off-balance. If so, it had certainly succeeded. She and Craig were caged together like prisoners who didn't know the length of their sentence. Increasingly, there were times when the confinement was too close for comfort. Jane's temper began to suffer and the night-life offered no comfort. Evenings out, however, probably were the safest option—an intimate dinner for two at home with Craig was as good a definition as any of playing with fire, and she wasn't fool enough yet to take risks on quite that scale. The entertainment value of the high life, though, was fading fast.

They came in from a show late one night. Both were tired; they'd hardly exchanged a word on the way home. As they walked upstairs, Jane heard the phone ring. She sighed wearily and turned automatically towards the living-room. At least half the calls lately had been for her.

'Don't worry, I'll get it,' said Craig. 'It's probably some nocturnal nuisance dialling this number at random.' He picked up the receiver as she hesitated in the doorway, wondering if she could just say goodnight and go on up to her own room. 'Yes?' An odd expression crossed his face and he looked up at her. She waited. 'Yes, I'm delighted to hear you too. Just a moment, I'll get her.' He turned to Jane. 'It's for you. Long-distance.' He sounded, for the first time in hours, amused.

'Me?' Puzzled, she took the instrument. 'Hello?' she asked hesitantly.

'Darling!' A familiar and long-unheard voice assaulted her. 'I found your message on the answer-phone the other day and I've been trying to get hold of you ever since. Tell me *all* about it.'

She sat down, weakly, remembering the mixture of irritation and relief she had felt at being greeted by an automated voice and a cheerful invitation to 'have a nice day' on the two occasions she had attempted this call. 'Hello, Mother,' she said with a combination of humour and resignation. 'Have you got the time difference wrong again? It's after midnight here.'

'Never mind that. I want to hear all about this Craig of yours.'

She looked up. 'Her' Craig could obviously hear every word; he was looking far too pleased. 'Go away,' she mouthed at him.

He blew her a kiss and walked out, saying, 'Give her my love.'

Jane ignored him and turned her attention back to her mother's enthusiastic interrogation. She had evidently been finding out about Craig, and seemed to approve of what she had learned.

'Do you know how much he's worth?' she demanded.

'No.' Jane suspected she soon would.

Her mother quoted a figure that made her blink before adding, 'Not that that's much by Texas standards, but it's certainly a very nice start. Now, I've seen a newspaper cutting, but you can't tell from those things. Is he really that good-looking?'

She should ask Sally; Jane was getting fed up with Craig's good looks. She didn't *need* to be told of his effect on women: she was all too aware of it herself.

'Very,' she said aloud. She wondered if he was listening on the upstairs extension. Her tone would probably amuse him.

'You don't sound very enthusiastic, dear. Are you sure everything's all right?'

For one instant, Jane wanted to tell her mother every detail of the mess she was in: the mockery of an engagement, the absurd threatening letter, even the stupid feelings that to Craig were just chemistry and which she didn't want to analyse at all. She wanted to cry. But she wasn't the crying type, and she'd got out of the habit of confiding in her mother a dozen years ago.

She tried to sound more cheerful. 'Of course I'm all right. It's just that it's the middle of the night here and I'm a bit tired, that's all. Craig asked me to send you his love,' she added. She hadn't heard him come back into the room, and her back was to the door, but she knew he was there.

'You go to bed, then. Be sure and phone me tomorrow some time, and don't forget to let me know when you've set the date. Ben and I and your brother will be over for the wedding.'

'That's great.' She felt hollow as the ripples of deception spread yet wider. 'Give my love to Ben and the family. I'll phone at noon—your time,' she added firmly as she cradled the receiver.

She sat looking at it for a moment, then two long, elegant hands dropped gently on her shoulders, easing away the tension which knotted her neck muscles. It was very soothing and for a few moments she just let her head droop, allowing his fingers to work their magic. But relaxation could turn all too easily to something more dangerous, and she couldn't cope with anything else tonight.

'Thanks,' she said, sitting up. 'That, as you know, was my very sweet and totally disorganised mother.' She shook her head. 'She knows every detail of your income, has managed to find a photo of you, and still can't work out the time-difference for a call to England.' She shrugged and yawned. 'I suppose Ben did the research for her.'

'It's a pity he didn't place the call. You're dead on your feet: go to bed.' His voice was unexpectedly sympathetic and for a moment, as she let him pull her to her feet, she allowed herself to lean against him as though absorbing some of his apparently inexhaustible energy. Then she straightened.

'I'm going. Black rings under my eyes would never fit the image of the glamorous photographer's fiancée, would they? Or would you get credit for a night of passion?' Her waspish attack surprised even her, and she didn't feel any better about it when he just pushed her towards the door.

'Bed. Alone. Your own. I'm not even going to attempt to seduce someone who's two-thirds asleep, so don't provoke me. Go on, I'll lock up downstairs.

Had that really been what she was doing? She didn't know, or even care. As usual, he was right: what she needed was sleep. She stumbled into her room and shut the door.

She was still depressed when she woke next day. She eyed the heavy topaz ring on the table by the bed as though it were some medieval ball and chain holding her mercilessly in a situation she should never have accepted. She shut her eyes. It was no use. She was still here, still engaged to Craig Stanton, and still wondering whether she wouldn't be better off in a padded cell somewhere.

Eyes still closed, she reviewed the past week. She must have been mad to let herself be talked into this situation—but had there ever been a choice? Craig had manoeuvred her into it because of a debt he imagined he owed her, but she was beginning to think the situation had more dangers than the anonymous letter-writer who had shown no further signs of life. Never had she felt such an emotional see-saw. Sometimes Craig's companionship, their shared humour, his irreverent outlook and relaxed approach to life, exhilarated her, but he had only to look at her, raise a quizzical eyebrow, brush back that sun-streaked hair in an achingly familiar gesture, or even turn suddenly so that he caught her unawares, and she was snared again by the tug of the physical attraction which linked them.

He had never made any secret of wanting her and he surely—since Athens—could not doubt the way she responded to him; but physical appeal was not, and never could be, enough. But what else had he ever offered?

She didn't doubt that he felt the appeal too. His unpredictable temper and growing moodiness were not just the result of the pressure of work, she was convinced. Until last night there had been moments when she had feared that the increasing tension between them might snap his self-control. If he had offered any warmer sympathy then, she ruefully acknowledged, there was more than a chance she would not now be waking up in this room. The knowledge that, this time, she owed her safety to *his* restraint was a puzzle she couldn't work out.

Since she had met him she had learned how powerful sexual attraction could be; now she was finding that there were things to like and admire in Craig, too. It brought her dangerously close to waters in which she knew she could not safely swim.

Luckily, as the opening of the exhibition drew closer, she saw less of him than ever. Even their evenings out were curtailed as he worked downstairs far into the night. Her own article on Greek travel and holidays was completed and despatched and she had little opportunity in the circumstances to seek material for another, but she had learned one thing at least from the events of that night; she was her own worst enemy where Craig was concerned. Next time he might not be so forbearing. Right now boredom was infinitely safer than confrontation.

She could not, however, avoid the preview of the exhibition. Nor did she want to. He hadn't let her see any of the work that was being shown and she looked forward to seeing it on public display. To be going to the preview as his fiancée was something of an embarrassment, even though she was becoming used to the public side of the role at least, but she couldn't suppress a sense of pride in him whenever she thought of the approaching evening.

Originally, he had been going to come back from setting things up in the gallery to collect her. She was unsurprised, however, to receive a call from him to tell her that, thanks to the efforts of some 'ham-fisted bureaucrat', a last-minute hitch in the arrangements meant that he couldn't get away. He'd arranged a taxi, though.

'I'll see you about seven-thirty,' he said.

'I'm looking forward to it,' she told him honestly. It was more than she could have said of some of their more recent outings.

He chuckled. 'I hope you like what you see. I'll be interested in your comments. See you later.'

'See you.' She put the phone down. He sounded suspiciously cheerful, despite the ham-fisted bureaucrat. She didn't believe the last remark: if he'd wanted her opinion, couldn't he have shown her the pictures days ago instead of being so secretive?

She decided to arrive late. She wanted a chance to be part of the crowd, at least for a while, and to look at the pictures anonymously without having to play the role of doting fiancée. If she arrived too early, there might not be many people around.

The exhibition was in a new, very elegant Bond Street gallery. It was certainly popular: the three rooms were busy when she got there, with small groups of people pausing and commenting as they wandered around. Jane knew she shouldn't be annoyed by the trivial chatter she overheard, and she certainly had no right to the vaguely possessive attitude to his work which she seemed to have acquired. But that made no difference.

The pictures, however, were stunning. She found herself absorbed in the evidence of his stay in the Middle East: cities, scenery, people. Above everything else, she kept coming back to the people. She could almost breathe the atmosphere of the place, sense the moods of its inhabitants. She stepped back to see a photo of a group of peasant women, their backs bent in toil but faces vibrant with life, more clearly. She almost bumped into two men who seemed more absorbed in their drinks and conversation than in the pictures. They took no notice of her but Jane, her concentration broken, couldn't help overhearing part of what they were saying.

'Impressive, isn't he?' one of them commented.

'Very. He's even better than he was at the last show I saw,' the other agreed, to Jane's quiet pleasure. Then, in an entirely different voice and with an unpleasantly knowing expression, the man added, 'I wonder where he found the girl?'

His friend chuckled, evidently agreeing with his companion's unspoken assessment of the unknown model. 'Quite taking in her way, isn't she? Even if she's not his usual style. I hope she's tough—you know what he can be like.' He sounded almost admiring.

The answering laugh was rueful. 'If I don't, my sister does. It took her months to get back to normal. Silly fool,' he added dispassionately.

Jane was tempted to agree. The exchange reminded her of a side of Craig she would rather not think about. It had also aroused her curiosity. This room was full of pictures of remote places and people; it would be interesting to see what he did with someone who was deliberately posing for him. She eased her way through the crowd to the further room.

She looked round the small collection which filled one wall, and at the two portraits which dominated another, and wondered whether to swear, laugh, or run. Was this his revenge for her interference? Each flippant gesture, every parody of a pose, every laughing attitude she had assumed in Syntagma Square, seemed to be on display. It could, she realised, only be a selection, but never had she felt so ruthlessly exposed. The only mercy was the absence of whatever ghastly snaps those giggling idiots had taken of them together.

The two bigger pictures were, in a way, more disturbing. She had *thought* he had been up to something when she woke on the ferry. Now she knew. He had clearly been far more alert than she would have thought possible, remembering that very genuine illness.

In one shot he had caught her bundled and almost invisible in her bulky clothes, her back to him, only one hand showing, clutching at her own shoulder as if to ward off the night's chill. It was both anonymous and intimate, conveying a sort of defensive loneliness which she found uncomfortable to look at. The other was worse. She had evidently turned over. Still asleep, she had relaxed, her hand now limp and open on her lap almost, she realised, as if expecting the clasp of a lover. Her face was young and vulnerable.

She wanted to hide. It seemed impossible that no one here had yet identified her. Her face, she knew, was scarlet with appalled recognition. Then embarrassment faded fast, driven out by anger. Her interference might have been naïve and annoying, but it was a private dispute between Craig and herself. This was public humiliation. When she next saw him she was going to dismember him. Slowly.

A hand touched her shoulder. 'Like them?' asked an amused voice.

She kept a tight rein on herself. She did not wheel round and hit him, partly because—even in her fury—she suspected he would be unchivalrous enough to duck, or hit her back. She turned slowly and looked at him, searching for words. Despite herself, her breath caught in her throat and her pulse beat faster.

She ought to be used to it by now. She had seen him dressed formally often enough, but that effortless elegance and the sheer sense of *life* in him always caught her unprepared. He looked down at her, humour lurking in the twist of his mouth, and she thought she also caught a glimpse of satisfaction. He was evidently enjoying the situation she found herself in.

Around them, a bustle and a whispering was beginning. Everyone knew Craig, and it sounded as though her identity was circulating fast. Not that it mattered; if he wanted a scene, she wouldn't stop him. But perhaps it would be more satisfying to surprise him.

'Don't I get a model's fee?' she managed sweetly, her anger still simmering.

That laugh, which had delighted her in Athens, made heads turn here. The slight constraint that had held him relaxed as he saluted her poise.

'My models generally volunteer,' he told her.

'This was a special request,' she reminded him. 'No one mentioned publicity.'

'It was irresistible,' he admitted.

'It's a mistake,' she warned him and saw a wariness come into his eyes. 'Can we discuss it—or shall we have a slanging match?' she offered.

His gaze reassessed her mood. This time she wasn't going to give way. He'd had no right to do this to her and no amount of flattery or charm was going to improve the situation. If he didn't move soon it would give her great pleasure to throw the heavy ring in his face and storm out of the gallery. With any luck the combined operations should give both him and Toby headaches.

He wasn't a fool. He gestured to a door behind them. 'We can go in there,' he told her.

'Are they for sale?' she demanded, even before the door had shut behind them.

'No.' His voice was quiet, his eyes watchful. He couldn't have missed her relief at that minor reprieve. 'You'll probably also be pleased to hear that those two girls were worse than the usual amateurs—they didn't take anything worth printing.'

'That's irrelevant,' she dismissed, knowing he would not have shown someone else's work anyway. She could feel glad about it on a more private level later. It was the present situation that angered her. 'It's bad enough having the ones you took plastered all over the walls out there,' she said bitterly, not trying to hide her resentment. Her hands were clenched in anger and she carefully straightened them. 'Don't you care a thing about anyone's feelings but your own? And don't bother to answer,' she snapped when he seemed about to say something. 'I should know, shouldn't I? You involve me in your wretched spying, you force me into a farce of an engagement—and now *this*!' she told him explosively, all her resentment surfacing.

His own expression hardened. 'You involved yourself,' he reminded her harshly. 'And if you think I'm enjoying this situation any more than you are, you can think again.'

'Then it's about time your friend Toby got his act together and did something,' she retorted.

'Now there I agree with you. This whole mess can't end fast enough for me.'

Why should that hurt? It was what she wanted, too, wasn't it?

'Then let's go back outside and have this row publicly,' she challenged. '*That* should give us an excuse to go our separate ways, shouldn't it?' And then, because it was what was really hurting, she demanded, 'Did you *have* to get your own back quite so publicly? I might have annoyed you in Greece—I didn't humiliate you.'

His gaze narrowed and some of his exasperation seemed to leave him. 'At the time,' he admitted, '"Annoyed" was an understatement. And you know damn well why we can't end this charade yet. Besides,' he added more calmly, 'you're wrong about the pictures.'

She raised what she hoped was a sceptical brow. 'I haven't just seen my face wallpapering a gallery?' she asked with heavy sarcasm. 'You weren't hanging around to see my reaction?' She might want to hit him, but she wasn't going to risk it without a hundred yards start. Probably not even then: he was too skilled at getting his own back.

'No, you saw all that,' he agreed, 'and congratulations on your unexpected self-control out there, by the way. I was half hoping for something in the fireworks line.' He didn't know how nearly he had got it. And he wasn't safe now. He went on, in the same light voice, 'Anyway, the revenge *was* purely private—strictly between you and me. What the public is seeing are some damn good photographs. Not my usual style, perhaps, but I was pleased with the way they turned out—you photograph very well, you know. You don't think I'd have let them go on show if they hadn't been good enough, do you?' he added with sudden severity.

Oddly enough, she believed him. He did take his work seriously. It didn't, however, make her any more comfortable with the idea of the pictures. He seemed to sense her reservations. 'Go and look at them again,' he recommended. 'Try to pretend they have nothing to do with you; just judge them as you would the others.'

'No, thanks.' That sort of detachment was just not hers. Besides, she had no intention of going out there again. 'I'm going home.'

'Home?' he queried sharply.

She had meant the Chelsea house, but it would be marvellous to be able to go back to the privacy of her own place. For a moment she toyed wistfully with the idea, then she sighed in defeat. There really was no option but to see this through to the end. However bitter. 'To your home,' she clarified. 'Your show's probably brilliant, but I've suddenly lost my enthusiasm. You can make whatever excuses for me that you like.' She turned away from him, but then swung back with momentarily renewed anger. 'Couldn't you at least have *asked* me?' she demanded.

He was very still, watching her. 'Would you have agreed?' His voice was unapologetic.

'No,' she admitted.

'I thought not. You don't seem particularly keen to be photographed. That's why I didn't ask you, the pictures deserve to be shown. You may not want to look at them, but those people out there...' his gesture indicated the crowd beyond the shut door '...aren't laughing at them.'

'Neither am I,' she said bleakly. 'And I still want to leave.' Whatever he said, she felt rawly exposed by those pictures. She knew how merciless his camera could be and had no wish at all to see whatever inadequacies he might have revealed.

His gaze rested on her thoughtfully; she stared back, defiant. 'I'll arrange a cab,' he said curtly, and left the room.

Without him, the tension drained away, leaving her limp with reaction. Perhaps, if there was no one else around, she *would* like another look at the pictures. But not tonight.

He managed to find both a taxi and a rear entrance to the gallery so that she was spared having to go back through the crowd again. She didn't hear him come in later that night, possibly because she was too involved in her own thoughts. It still made no sense to her; Jillian would have been delighted to pose for him, she was certain. A face like hers would look stunning to almost any camera, let alone Craig's. He must surely have used her as a model in the past? But the photos of her, Jane, were the only portraits—except the Middle East ones— on display. She didn't understand it. And she hated to think what the reviewers were going to say.

What the papers had to say was universally enthusiastic. 'A major talent' was a phrase which came up more than once. There was some division in preference between the Middle Eastern pictures and those of her, but no one seemed inclined to mock. Jane shook her head and pushed the papers away, half relieved and half convinced the world had run mad. She didn't say anything to Craig about the reviews and he made no further comment on her reaction to the pictures. In fact they didn't say much to each other at all. An uneasy calm remained in operation as they managed to avoid each other fairly successfully for almost two days. It was on the afternoon of the second day that Craig decided to end the stalemate.

Jane had been staring listlessly at a blank notepad, pretending to work, when she heard the sharp rap on the door. It could only be Craig, and she felt more relief then irritation that he had sought her out.

'Come in,' she called, unable to suppress the lifting of her spirits. It had been a long two days.

A familiar figure in old jeans and a dark blue shirt lounged in the doorway, a quizzical smile touching his lips. 'I've two tickets for that new musical you wanted to see,' he told her. 'Can we call a truce and enjoy ourselves for a change?' he wondered.

She pretended to consider. 'Well, I suppose we ought to celebrate your show's triumph.' If he was offering an olive-branch, why should she be ungenerous? Then, capitulating entirely, she smiled happily. 'I'd love to go.'

He seemed almost as pleased as she was. 'Great. We'll make a night of it.'

And they did. They dined early at the restaurant where he had taken her when they became engaged, then went on to the theatre. He'd taken a box for them and they enjoyed the first half in comfort and luxury. The show was as good as Jane had hoped and Craig was an entertaining, if irreverent, companion. Best of all, no one seemed in the least interested in their engagement. Until the interval.

They had ordered drinks and were waiting at the bar when the tall, slender, dark-haired girl swayed up to Craig. She was everything Jane knew she was not; she was also familiar. Jillian Shaw. Tonight she wore a red, almost backless dress with the confidence of someone who knew her figure was flawless. She didn't even seem to see Jane.

Moving between them so that Jane was forced to take a step back, Jillian put one hand confidentially on Craig's shoulder. Red nails glimmered against the dark cloth. The vague pity Jane had felt the other night evaporated fast in the face of the other's assurance, even if it was fairly evident that she had found some of it in a bar several drinks ago.

Jillian leaned closer to Craig who was looking at her with a sort of amused tolerance. Jane noted that he made no effort to move away. Around them she saw suppressed smiles and looks aimed at Craig that might be slightly envious. All the pleasure she had felt in the evening faded rapidly. Drunk or sober, the other girl had all the advantages.

Over the head that was now resting on his shoulder, Craig's eyes met Jane's. His were rueful, possibly entertained, but for once she felt no answering humour. The suggestion of intimacy between these two, first made by Toby, was being confirmed in front of her and she felt slight, insignificant and uncertain. Not unnaturally, anger was her first reaction.

She might just have walked off back to her seat if Jillian had not lifted her head lazily from its resting-place and said, looking down at her from dark, almond-shaped eyes, 'Perhaps you'd better introduce me to your little fiancée after all, darling. She always seems to be around, somehow.'

Craig, still watching Jane, smiled. 'I've noticed the same thing myself.'

It was a slap in the face. A minute's thought might have—as it did much later—made her wonder whether he had expected her to be amused by shared memories of the ferry and Athens, but by then it was too late. Their drinks had arrived.

Picking up the tall, frosted glass, Jane turned, letting the high heel of one shoe catch in the carpet's luxurious pile. The drink—ice, wine and soda—cascaded down Jillian's naked back.

The piercing shriek which made every other head turn didn't even make Jane flinch. Returning Craig's bland regard with an even stare of her own, she turned and walked off to their box. Behind her she heard a bustle of activity and a shrill, querulous voice raised in half-hysterical distress. She almost expected to feel the red talons sink themselves into the back of her neck and was quietly relieved to regain the relative security of her seat.

Would he be furious? Possibly. She probably shouldn't blame him. Perhaps he thought she was putting on the sort of devoted fiancée act that Toby had seemed to expect. If anything, that would be worse. She didn't think she could cope if he congratulated her on the perfor-mance. She certainly didn't feel like apologising; this time, Jillian had asked for it.

He rejoined her surprisingly quickly. Gravely he offered a tall glass.

'I thought you might like a replacement,' he ex-plained, smiling.

Imperceptibly, she relaxed. She had no intention, though, of asking whether it was she or Jillian who was entertaining him.

'I thought cold liquids were good for hysteria,' she justified her action as she accepted the drink.

He considered this. 'You're probably right, but they're generally applied after, not before, the event. Besides...' his lips twitched as he lounged in the chair next to her, looking out towards the stage '...one of the ice-cubes proved very hard to recover.'

Perhaps she should be feeling sorry for Jillian after all. 'I'm surprised you didn't stay to assist,' she commented. She'd given him all the excuses he needed, hadn't she? She wasn't feeling at all proud of herself by now. It had been too easy to stoop to the other girl's level.

Craig was shaking his head. 'Too much competition. I don't like crowds.' He sounded indifferent, adding in the same offhand tone, 'My tastes are altogether more exclusive.'

The applause which greeted the return of the orchestra saved her, probably fortunately, from asking to have that remark explained. But it lingered in her mind: if he was referring to her, how was she meant to take it? This evening, for once, he was keeping his distance, not even taking the opportunity afforded by the box to flirt with her as he had done so often before. Oddly enough, she found the restraint as difficult to cope with as the provocation. Sometimes she wondered if she knew anything about her own mind any more.

The second half of the musical was far less entertaining than the first. She had too much time to wonder at the savagery of her own emotions when she had heard Jillian call Craig 'darling', and the probably unworthy satisfaction she had felt when he had come back to the box so quickly. She had to keep reminding herself that this engagement was only an act, like those figures cavorting on the stage in front of her, and that the final curtain would come down for her, too. Soon.

CHAPTER EIGHT

'JILLIAN said her dress was ruined,' Craig informed Jane idly over coffee and toast next morning.

'What a pity.' Even in the light of the new day, she found she didn't feel particularly repentant, and she had no intention at all of trying to work out what that might mean. She was discovering that self-analysis was a business which seldom offered any comfortable conclusions. At least last night's exhibition seemed to have had one beneficial effect: that mounting strain between Craig and herself had eased.

Craig raised an eyebrow at her lack of interest. 'Am I going to have to issue a health warning about you before we go out again?' The prospect didn't seem to worry him

'Probably,' she agreed, 'unless you have a cure for boredom.' It wasn't his problem, but he was at least partly responsible for the current situation and anyway, there was no one else who, as a newly engaged woman, she could grumble about boredom to. She gestured vaguely. 'This is all very luxurious, and the cloak and dagger stuff would probably seem utterly fascinating on a film, but it does get a bit tedious after a while. Having you as a nanny,' she added, not without deliberate malice, 'isn't exactly how I saw my first steps in an independent career.' She reached for another piece of toast.

'A nanny!' He sounded disgusted. 'What a revolting idea!'

'That's what I mean,' she agreed. 'What do you suggest I do about it?'

'Sack me?' he offered, still apparently trying to come to terms with being seen as a nursery tyrant.

'I'd like to,' she admitted. Perhaps they might stand a chance if they could only get out of this unnatural situation they were in. Until then, humour might be her best protection. Or something useful to do. 'But aren't you forgetting the nasty little letter-writer?' she reminded him.

He echoed her. 'I'd like to. But I suppose we can't guarantee that he'll feel the same way.' She glimpsed his exasperation—it sounded almost as bad as her own. He paused, giving her discontent apparently serious consideration. 'Why don't you use the current situation? Write something about the glamour of society night-life—or its absence.'

It wasn't even worth considering. She'd rejected it days ago. 'People already know more than they want to about it—both its delights and its emptiness, depending on who you consult.'

His wry smile accepted her implied verdict on the *milieu* he moved in and she remembered his escapes, to America or a Greek ferry, and realised that it probably wasn't where he would normally choose to spend his life. Not for the first time, she accepted that part of his charm was that she never had to explain herself to him. Had Jillian felt the same way?

He had been thinking, apparently, 'I suppose I do have an alternative suggestion,' he began with a hint of reluctance.

'Yes?' She was cautious, but anything was better than sitting around and doing nothing. Except thinking.

'You could work for—or with—me,' he said carefully, his expression neutral.

She had grown used to seeing him with a camera, resigned to the fact that it was sometimes pointed in her direction, had even begun to forgive him for the exhibition, but she had no intention of making a career of it. People like Jillian Shaw were models.

'I don't want to pose for you,' she said with what she hoped sounded like casual indifference.

'I wasn't going to ask you to,' he retorted. Evidently he hadn't forgotten her reaction to the show.

Absurd to feel rejected. She wouldn't have done it if he'd asked, would she? 'So what *do* you want me to do?'

She didn't need the long pause: the glint in his eye and the twitch of his lips gave her the answer she'd invited. She was both irritated and relieved when he didn't exploit his advantage. He even seemed to hesitate. Eventually, he continued. 'It's just possible that you might be able to help me with the book about the Middle East that my agent is demanding. He liked the last one— and its sales—and is determined to *love* this one,' he added without any enthusiasm at all.

It didn't make sense. Jane couldn't see where she came in at all. Surely he didn't want a secretary? She remembered *Voyages* and her reaction to it. If the exhibition was anything to go by, his talent had increased since then: the new book was bound to be terrific. She had every intention of getting hold of a copy as soon as it was published—and no intention of admitting that to Craig.

'So what's the problem?' she asked.

'The problem,' he told her with evident irritation, 'is that this time he wants a text along with the pictures.' It seemed quite straightforward. She let the silence grow until his exasperation exploded. 'I can't do it!' he admitted. 'I don't even *want* to do it. Either my pictures say what I want them to say, or I'm silent. When I start trying to put things into words they sound like the worst sort of tourist guide or, even more horribly, unbearably sentimental.' He shuddered as though at a recent memory. Yes, Craig would be horrified by anything approaching sentiment.

She couldn't really believe the scale of the problem, but she was enjoying his frustration. 'It sounds tricky,' she said with a cautious sympathy.

'Oh, stop laughing at me, woman,' he snapped impatiently. 'Just try to imagine yourself having to rely on your holiday snapshots to tell others how you felt about your first visit to Delphi, and you'll see my problem.'

It was an uncomfortably accurate comparison. She *did* see what he meant. Her own photographs were so banal that, a couple of years ago, she had nearly given up taking a camera on holiday. She still rarely used it. Her journal made a far more atmospheric record of her experiences.

'So what are you suggesting?' she asked more seriously.

'That you write the text, of course,' he said as though it should have been blindingly obvious.

She was stunned. 'But I don't know a thing about the Middle East!' she protested.

'You don't have to. It's the pictures that need the commentary: I can give you any facts you need. And don't tell me you can't do it. I read your article on Greece—ferry travel and all—and it was good.'

Surprised pleasure caught her unawares, softening her instinctive resistance to his idea. She hadn't given him the piece. She hadn't even told him it had been published. He must have taken some trouble to get hold of it. 'Thank you,' she said, disconcerted.

'Don't thank me—help me out,' he retorted, his smile ruefully acknowledging the improbability of his actually *asking* for assistance.

That was why, after some more increasingly weak argument from herself, they had come to spend afternoons together sorting through, and selecting from, hundreds of photographs. They were so impressive that at first she wanted to include everything, but he was far more ruthless and eventually some sort of sequence began to emerge.

At first she had just taken notes of what he had said about the location or circumstances of each shot, but she soon realised that that was not enough. She would have to interview him, ask questions that he didn't want to answer and provoke a real response, and then select her text from what he revealed.

When she first produced the cassette recorder he raised an eyebrow. 'Is that necessary?' he demanded.

'It is if you want a decent text,' she told him bluntly. 'Or are you really just giving me something to do to ward off boredom?'

That was as far as the protest got. He obviously hated knowing that he was being recorded, but professionalism made him accept her decision.

Over the next few days she found that her questioning produced a disconcerting result. Grudgingly, he began to show the strain of feeling in him that was only present uninhibitedly in the pictures themselves. That he was affected by her probing was evident. She came to expect his foulest moods and nastiest comments after they had been looking at the most poignant episodes. It was then, too, that she felt most vulnerable to him and found it increasingly hard to go on with a job that was proving fascinating as well as disturbing.

She was surprised to find little political comment in the pictures: he seemed exclusively concerned with the sufferings and triumphs of individuals. What he clearly hated was any implication by her that the sensitivity of the photography said anything at all about him.

'I'm just the eye behind the lens, not some moral crusader or bleeding heart,' he told her sharply when she commented on a particularly heart-rending image.

She ignored that. Readers would draw their own conclusions. Then she grinned, and picked up another shot.

This one showed a joyful moment, not a harrowing one. A couple, newly married, were standing looking at each other in a rather drab, modern street, litter blowing behind them and rubbish accumulating around the run-down concrete block of flats. The blaze of love in the looks the young people were exchanging, captured by Craig, reduced the tawdry surroundings to insignificance.

'For a man who doesn't rate love very highly, you've managed to photograph it rather well,' she observed.

He flicked the picture dismissively with one finger. 'I was lucky with the light,' he told her. 'Besides, the trick is not to go back a year later and see the illusion shattered.'

Well, what had she expected? 'You won't get the chance to do that in this case,' she reminded him.

'True enough. I'll steer clear of the whole area for a while: there are plenty of other places to explore.'

For a moment, his eyes had a faraway look as though he were contemplating his next journey. Jane could just see him picking up the old duffle bag and his precious cameras and being gone in a couple of hours. The tan was beginning to fade, but he still looked slightly exotic. The fine-drawn good looks and habitual air of detachment could be both forbidding and attractive. She should know. She looked quickly down at her notes to hide anything her face might betray.

She pushed the 'record' button on the cassette player. 'Shall we get on?' she asked briskly.

'Why not?' he agreed, sounding far too good-humoured.

The pictures were marvellous. It was probably fortunate, however, that whenever admiration began to surface too evidently he managed to infuriate her.

She was looking one afternoon at a picture of a home devastated by flood following on drought; a man contemplating the ruins of his past and the bleak future of the small boy who clung to his tattered trousers.

'You must include that,' she insisted.

'Effective, isn't it? Give them a couple of days and the man will be convincing every gullible tourist that he's deaf, blind and leprous, while the kid makes do with looking soulful. They might even find begging more profitable than scratching at the soil for a living. Of course, in a few years the brat could be making a very good living indeed from the more romantic middle-aged females who like to explore exotic slums; he'll grow up very pretty indeed.' His voice was harshly dismissive. All she could hear was a cynical disillusion that almost hurt. She dropped the picture.

'It doesn't have to go in,' she said.

He moved it from the large heap of discards to the smaller pile of accepted photographs. 'Oh, yes, it does. You may not like my image of ten years hence; rejecting the picture won't stop it happening.'

'I thought you weren't a crusader?' she challenged. Had he been, once?

'I'm not, but it's a damn good picture. Stop being sentimental.'

With difficulty, she did so, and moved on to the next image. She avoided commenting on the fact that it showed the elegantly shod feet of the wealthy trampling heedlessly past the outstretched and crippled hand of a beggar. Doubtless he could say something cynical about that, too. It didn't alter the fact that his lens had seen what most took for granted and ignored. She dropped it on the smaller heap without comment.

She wasn't sorry when he drew the session to an early close and stood up, stretching.

'I have to go out,' he told her abruptly.

It was the first she'd heard of it. 'To the exhibition?' she assumed.

'No.' She didn't think he was going to say anything else. He sounded irritable, obviously resenting her curiosity. 'I thought I'd go and look at something a little more cheerful than these.' He gestured at the heaped pictures. 'A friend of mine has a new model on his books and he wants to persuade me to take some publicity shots.'

'But you don't do that sort of thing, do you?' She was surprised.

'If it's any business of yours: not usually. But I don't mind admiring the scenery for a few hours,' he went on, his voice almost hostile. 'Do I have to account for *all* my movements to you?'

'No, of course not,' she protested, adding gloomily, 'but I don't see why you get to gad about and have fun while I'm stuck in here.'

'I hardly think Larry's new model would be very welcoming if I brought you along.' He was bored, his expression making it clear she was being tiresome. 'Besides, you agreed to stay put.'

'I didn't think it was going to be such a one-sided affair,' she grumbled.

Something flickered in his eyes. 'It's not an affair at all,' he pointed out coldly.

Was that the problem? She didn't believe it; she had a very clear idea of what the unknown Larry's model would be like. Craig wasn't staying to argue. In fact, he wasn't staying at all.

'Will you be back this evening?' she called to his retreating figure.

'I haven't the faintest idea,' he said without pausing. 'Don't wait up.' Amazing how nasty a conventional phrase could sound. She heard the quick steps on the stairs, the slam of the front door and a car driving away.

She resisted the temptation to watch from the living-room window. She didn't know what was wrong with Craig, or what had triggered the sudden and moody departure but she *did* know what was wrong with herself, and she didn't like it at all. Jealousy, she was learning, left a particularly nasty taste in the mouth.

Well, she wasn't going to sit around all afternoon and savour it. Since there was no other project available, she would get on with this one. She began to replay the cassettes she had recorded, pausing occasionally to make notes or put the selected pictures tentatively in some sort of order.

It took hours but, with only a break to make a rather incoherent and unconvincing call to Texas, which left her mother asking questions Jane didn't want to answer and seeming improbably optimistic about the idea of marriage, she stuck to it. Even without Craig's magnetic physical presence, his voice still had the power to affect her, but she tried to listen with detachment. Behind the veneer of cynicism and indifference that marked so many of his comments, and which she found it so difficult to cope with, she began to hear something else. Anger. It was the anger of someone who had repeatedly tried and failed to make things different and could now only reveal them as they were. When the situation was most tragic, his offhand flippancy was most in evidence. Did he *need* cynicism to ward off the vulnerability of pity? She remembered his casual account of an emotionally under-privileged childhood. He'd certainly never been encouraged to reveal his feelings. By now, he probably couldn't.

Afternoon drifted slowly towards evening and she went on with her notes. If she was right, she understood him a little better, but she didn't fool herself that that would make living with him any easier. Craig would *hate* to be understood. She giggled at the thought of his reaction if she even implied any such thing or, worse, behaved with understanding tolerance next time he was particularly cutting. It might even be worth trying, just to see his face.

'What's funny?'

She hadn't heard him come in, hadn't expected him back for hours. Photographs slithered from her fingers to the floor as she stood up from where she had been kneeling amid a scattered circle of notes and pictures. She blinked up at him. The foul mood seemed to have gone, but she was wary.

He surveyed the mess. 'You've been working hard,' he observed, 'but if you've managed to produce something comic, I'm a far worse photographer than I thought.'

'No, that's not what I was laughing at,' she admitted gesturing at the glossy black and white images. 'How could I?' Without giving him a chance to demand an alternative explanation, she went on. 'I think I've worked out the basic structure of the text. I'd hoped to get it organised enough to show you tomorrow. I didn't expect to see you again today.'

His laugh was rueful. 'You probably didn't want to.' As an apology, it was very oblique, but it was more than she had expected. Her surprise must have shown because his smile widened and he ran one hand through his hair, leaving it ruffled. Not for the first time she suppressed the urge to smooth it down.

He squatted easily among the organised chaos on the carpet, his rapid gaze quickly taking in what she had done. Picking up one page of notes, he scanned it. Jane found she was tense, awaiting his reaction, aware that she had wanted to be better prepared than this before she showed him anything. Her ideas were still very raw.

He put the page on one side, then picked up another, a slight frown of concentration creasing his forehead. She felt her nails digging into damp palms. Then he looked up, and there was no ridicule at all in his expression as he straightened.

'It's always a pleasure to be proved right,' he told her.

'There's still a lot to do——' she began.

'I can see that, but I meant that I was right to ask you to do it,' he interrupted, looking as though he was congratulating them both. 'I'd never have thought of doing it this way, but of course you're right, *and* I like the style. I unreservedly withdraw any cracks I might have made about sentimentality.'

She flushed slightly with relief and pleasure, but was still cautious. She didn't quite trust this mood. 'You've had a good afternoon?' she deduced.

He laughed. 'Not bad.'

'The model was entertaining?' Her pleasure was cooling fast.

'Not at all.' He sounded indifferent. 'There was nothing but a "Vacant" sign behind the classic profile.

After an hour, Larry and I left her happily exchanging glances with her own reflection in the nearest mirror and went out for a couple of drinks.'

They'd certainly done wonders for his mood. Her own improved markedly.

'I thought you might like a break from gaol,' he went on. 'What do you say to a drink and a meal at the pub?'

It sounded marvellous. 'You mean no showing-off or trying to convince the gossips, your friends and our enemies of our mutual devotion?'

'Exactly that. Come on, let's tidy this lot away and go out for a couple of hours. Do you feel brave enough to walk, or shall I order a taxi?'

'We're walking,' she decided firmly. She quickly picked up the notes and pictures, putting them carefully in a folder. 'I'll just take these upstairs and pull a comb through my hair, then I'll be with you.'

She almost ran up to her room, absurdly cheered by the improvement in Craig's temper. She put the folder on her desk and glanced at her own reflection. She was no model and saw nothing there to be complacent about, but there was a pleasant glow to her clear skin and her eyes held a sparkle in their tawny depths.

It only took twenty minutes to shower and change. A loosely pleated skirt in warm yellow and a stone-coloured cotton sweater over a matching shirt replaced the jeans and sweatshirt. She added a little lipstick and mascara to an otherwise unmade-up face and brushed her curls vigorously. Her hair needed cutting; it was beginning to tumble around her shoulders, although the length wasn't unflattering, she realised. It seemed to emphasise her cheekbones. She picked up her coat and hurried downstairs to Craig.

He made no comment on the time she had taken but paused as they passed his studio door on the way out.

'Hang on a minute,' he told her, opening its door. He came out a moment later with the Paisley shawl. 'Here. This should go well with that outfit.' He arranged it over the shoulders of her coat, his hands lingering imperceptibly. Over her head he regarded their linked reflections in the hall mirror. 'Yes, that's better. You'll have to hang on to it. It suits you.'

A pity she couldn't hang on to him, she thought. Would he suit her? Was this how others saw him? She touched the lovely fabric, seeing herself in the baroque-framed glass. He was right—it did look good. Her eyes met his in the mirror and she felt oddly shy. *They* looked good together. Or was that wishful thinking? 'Thank you,' she said, almost hesitantly, not quite convinced he meant it. And then, more normally as she remembered his parting gift in Athens, 'Are you determined to make sure I have enough scarves?'

He clearly had no trouble following her thoughts. 'Something like that. I couldn't face the ferry version again.' He took her hand. 'Come on, stop preening. I'm hungry.'

So was she, and mirrors could be disturbing things. She let him tug her towards the door.

They walked together to the end of the road and then turned right to the friendly wine bar that was the nearest thing to a pub in the area. It was only a couple of hundred yards away. There was an almost guilty pleasure in walking like this, she thought, flirting with a danger that seemed increasingly remote and unlikely with every day that passed.

'Have you heard anything from Toby recently?' she wondered aloud.

He seemed to have been thinking much the same as her. 'Nothing. It all seems slightly improbable at the moment, doesn't it? I don't suppose we'll get the details until it's all over.'

He sounded unconcerned, but Jane couldn't help wondering for just how much longer he'd be willing to endure the constraints of their ambiguous position. Of course, he'd probably put up with it while they worked on the book. At the moment, it seemed as though she was finding it more of a strain then he was.

For once his good mood seemed to be straightforward and enduring. Over a simple meal and a bottle of white wine they found it easy to talk about a wide variety of subjects. The conversation ranged haphazardly without discovering any of the hidden traps that so often lately seemed to have mined their encounters. It was a luxury to relax like this.

Unfortunately, they lingered too long over the last glass in the bottle. If only, Jane later thought, they had left the wine bar a few minutes earlier, the evening might have ended differently. They were arguing in a friendly way over nothing very important when she saw the door open and the tall, burly, dark-haired man she had almost bumped into in the gallery walked in.

She recognised him at once, and glanced away. It was too late. He had seen her and her companion and recognised them both. He strode over to their table.

'Craig!' he exclaimed. 'Where have you been hiding?'

Craig looked up, the animation fading from his face. 'Hello, David,' he said in a resigned tone. 'We haven't exactly been hiding, or don't you read these days?' He turned to Jane. 'This is David Shaw. We were at school together. David, you haven't met my fiancée, Jane Simpson, have you?'

'No. But I've seen the pictures.' He laughed a little too loudly and Jane wondered what bar he'd been in before he came here. 'The reality,' he told her with rather heavy gallantry, 'is even more entrancing.'

'Thank you,' she said coolly. She had so far got on well with most of Craig's friends; she had a feeling she might make an exception for David Shaw, Jillian's brother. He had sat down beside them and clearly intended to stay.

'Aren't you going to buy me a drink so that I can toast the happy couple?' he demanded. He leaned closer to Jane. 'Her glass is empty, too,' he noticed.

Craig stood up. 'We were just going, but I'll get you a drink. Another glass of wine, Jane?'

She opted for mineral water. There was a crush at the bar and Craig was away for several minutes. That was all the time it took for David to move rather too close and drape an arm confidingly round her shoulder.

'I'm not surprised he's put that rock on your finger,' he told her, slightly incoherently. 'Always did have an eye for quality, did Craig. Mind you, Jillian, that's my sister, wants to kill you,' he added gloomily. 'Just when I thought she was over him, she read about the engagement and now she's gone all weepy again. Now she says you insulted her, and he ignores her. Seems unlikely to me. You wouldn't do us both a good turn and swap him for me?' It was only clumsy teasing but he was drunker than she'd realised, and suddenly she found his nearness intolerable.

'Excuse me.' She stood up, shrugging him off. 'No, thanks. I'll stick with what I've got.' Which isn't much, she reflected. Jillian wouldn't have to drown her sorrows for much longer. She glanced over at the bar. Craig was just being served. 'Better still, I'll leave you two alone together to compare notes.'

Pulling her coat around her shoulders, she walked out of the bar, ignoring David's blurred protest. She stalked along the street, furious and humiliated. Would she be another 'silly fool' in David's casual gossip a few weeks from now?

It was only when she stood outside the closed front door of the house that she realised she had no key. Rage, this time against herself, threatened to overwhelm her. She wanted to kick the door down, instead she would have to return to the bar and face Craig's mockery and the leers of his wretched schoolfriend.

There was a step behind her and she whirled, suddenly afraid, reminded of all that had begun to seem foolish only a few hours ago.

Craig was standing there. He was holding out the key and his expression was grim. She took the key from him, opened the door and went upstairs. Neither of them said a word.

'Did he make a pass at you?' he demanded as they entered the living-room.

'Not really. He merely compared me with his sister and suggested I forsake you for him,' she told him.

Craig relaxed fractionally. 'I left him about to pass out in his Scotch, drowning in self-pity and muttering that some people had all the luck. What did he say about Jillian?'

'Nothing very flattering.'

'Well, at least she's now convinced that we're through. Even if it took an engagement to do it.' He sounded satisfied with this outcome, and something in Jane snapped.

'How nice for you. But if she's anything like Larry's little pet, or any of the other raving beauties who keep falling over your feet, then I doubt if she thinks anything of the sort. She's "seen the pictures", too, hasn't she?' Just like David.

'What do you mean?' He was suddenly intent, but she was past trying to interpret his moods.

She swung away from him. 'I mean that no one in their right minds probably understands why we're engaged. They're either laughing themselves silly, or laying bets on how long it will last. And they'll be right, won't they?'

A hand on her shoulder forced her to turn and look at him. She was fleetingly glad she was angry enough to conceal the tears that weren't very far away. His eyes were as clear and as hard as glass.

'You are a blind idiot,' he said carefully. His voice was cool, but there was nothing temperate about the fingers which dug into her shoulders. 'If anyone in London thinks our engagement is unconvincing, you must be the only one. I've never been so deluged in deeply sincere congratulations in my life; not even the first book got me as many good wishes as I've had in the past week. When it's all over, I'm likely to be lynched by every friend I used to have.' Carefully, he let her go and stepped back.

She ran her palms down her cheeks, not understanding. 'What do you mean?'

'You always dismiss compliments about your looks, don't you?' he asked.

She shrugged uncomfortably. 'Not really. But I don't have any illusions about them, if that's what you mean.'

'And everyone else has, I suppose? Why do you think Jillian is so determined to wish you out of existence?'

'Jealousy, I suppose.' She wished this interrogation was over. She just wanted to be alone.

'You suppose right. And it isn't the ring she's jealous of.' He turned aside for a moment, picking up a magazine she had left lying on a table, flicking through its pages until he came to the picture he wanted. 'I suppose this is the sort of face you think I ought to be photographing—or taking to bed?' His voice was savage.

She looked. The model was tall, elegant, poised. 'Why not?' She was bewildered now. 'It would make more sense.'

He dropped the magazine contemptuously to the floor. 'No, it wouldn't. Oh, I agree her bone-structure's good, she's got all the right features in the right places, but there's nothing else there. It's about as dynamic as a picture of rolling English farmland: very lovely, no doubt, but how boring can you get?'

'But——' He was watching her now, and she felt the blood pound in her face.

'But what about you?' He took a step towards her, and his voice softened slightly. 'You, my dear, innocent Jane, are as complex as a chess problem, with all the mystery and allure of the sea or a far mountain range. One look from those golden eyes and any man who isn't brain dead or blind would ache to know more, to find out if the maze of your hair is as soft and intricate as it looks.' His hands came up, almost reluctantly, to touch, then tangle in her hair. He went on, his eyes holding hers. 'Anyone knowing you would want to discover if your body is as enticingly feminine as it seems and if,' he added more harshly, 'silencing you could be even half as delightful as the prospect of it.'

Her lips parted in protest, but he stopped her with one finger against her them.

'You are also, without doubt, the most infuriating, interfering woman it has ever been my dubious pleasure to meet.' Anger, as though he resented his own desire, tinged his voice and the hand that tightened in her hair was no longer gentle, nor was the arm around her waist which drew her hard against him.

The kiss was almost brutal. His mouth ravished hers as though he had to punish her for making him want her. His lips moved over hers till they parted on a sobbing breath. She felt herself being taken over as, without breaking the kiss, he pushed her coat from her shoulders to the floor. She let it go, raising her own hands to his shoulders, mutely accepting the persuasions of his roving hands.

His mouth released hers, but only for long enough to tug her down beside her on the sofa, his hand pushing aside her jumper, finding the buttons of her blouse.

Abruptly, his urgency was hers. No longer merely submissive to his demands, she began to make her own explorations. He laughed softly, shrugging out of his jacket and taking the opportunity to remove her sweater entirely before pressing her back against the cushions. His hands brushed her hardening nipples lightly through the fabric of her blouse and it felt as though something electric passed through her.

'Craig!'

The exclamation and the moan that escaped her seemed to please him; he repeated the caress, taking her soft cry into his own mouth with lips that teased and provoked.

Then his hands were against her bare flesh. Her own palms stilled against him, accepting a pleasure that was close to pain, feeling him cup her breast with one of his long-fingered hands.

She fumbled with his shirt-buttons, trying to concentrate, knowing that somewhere she had just lost a battle, uncertain if she even cared. At last she was touching him, feeling the faint dampness of his skin, the thud of his heart beneath her hand which told of his own excitement. She twisted against him, wanting the pleasure of her lips against the warm skin. He cupped her head to him, drawing her into the curve of his body. She felt the full strength of his arousal as her own body caught fire.

His hand moved against her breast again, and she arched into the strength of his lean hips, her control shattered beyond repair. His was only slightly stronger. He released her with almost palpable reluctance, holding her upper body in a loose embrace although the intimate weight of his hips still held her trapped.

He dropped a light kiss on lips that felt swollen. His grey eyes, no longer cold or unreadable, scanned her face with urgent desire and something that she desperately wanted to believe was affection. He gave a slightly shaken chuckle, a ghost of the familiar laugh.

'Last chance, love. I'll count to five, and after that there's no way I'm letting you go. One...'

He was teasing, gently mocking her earlier resistance, expecting no response than the one she had already given without words. But he shouldn't have done it. She wanted to wake up tomorrow, blaming herself probably, but knowing it was too late. Now he was giving her a chance, and she couldn't ignore it and keep a shred of self-respect. Not that there was anything to be proud of in drawing back at the eleventh hour.

'. . . Three . . . four,' she heard.

'No.' She meant to sound forceful—it came out like a frightened croak.

He didn't believe her. 'No?' he queried gently, looking down at her half-naked body.

'No.' That was better. She didn't struggle. She sensed it wouldn't take much for him to ignore her refusal, using his far greater strength to override any protest. He must know she wouldn't fight him.

'Do you mean that?' There was a dangerous edge to the quiet voice.

'Yes. I'm sorry——' she began.

He rolled away from her and sat up, covering his face with his hands. 'Don't bother apologising. In fact, don't bother saying anything. Just get out. Now. While you still can,' he added, anger breaking through the iron restraint that showed in the white tension of his hands.

She went, picking up the more retrievable pieces of her clothing and abandoning the rest.

She didn't hear him come upstairs, didn't want to. She sat in bed, huddled in her most enveloping nightdress, shivering. It had been his words that had made her feel special, almost unique; they as much as his actions, had been her undoing. If for one moment longer she could have convinced herself that he meant them, she would have been downstairs with him now. Enjoying herself. She had no doubt about that: she had not known pleasure could be so intense, and she could still feel the demands of its fires flickering unsatisfied within her.

Then she remembered that it had been he who had let her go. That sort of consideration meant something, surely? The trouble was, she had no idea *what* it might mean. She only knew she was as far as ever from understanding Craig. Even worse was the growing fear that what she felt for him was something much more complicated than passion. To fall in love with him would, she told herself, be the worst of all possible mistakes. The only trouble with that, though, was the realisation that her own advice came far too late.

CHAPTER NINE

JANE didn't sleep well. Considering the torrid nature of her dreams, she wasn't sorry when her restlessness jerked her awake to lie staring into the empty blackness of the night. By the time the outline of the window was paling into a fuzzy pre-dawn greyness, she knew she wasn't going to sleep any more.

Getting up, she dressed quickly. For a while she occupied herself with the folder of photographs, extending her notes and organising her ideas. It probably wasn't the best way to stop herself thinking about Craig, but it was better than doing nothing and allowing her thoughts and memories to wander. Deliberately, she focused her attention on the relative merits of two striking pictures.

It was no good. She couldn't concentrate, and both pictures were equally good so they might as well both go in. Coffee, that was what she needed, she realised as she yawned and stretched stiff limbs. Coffee, and something to stop her thinking about last night.

She opened her door cautiously. At the end of the passage his was firmly shut and she could hear no sounds coming from the room beyond it. Barefoot, she trod quietly across the soft carpet and down the stairs, relieved when they didn't creak.

The living-room door was ajar. Feeling slightly safer, she walked in, thinking of coffee and wondering how she was going to get through the day. Then she stopped dead.

Craig was sprawled on the sofa, deeply asleep. His shirt was unbuttoned and his shoes were off, but he had made no effort to cover himself against the cold of the night. It was as though he had hardly moved since she had fled. Then she saw the half-empty bottle on the table beside him and the glass lying carelessly on its side as though it had fallen from his grasp.

Had she done that to him? In sleep he looked younger, curiously vulnerable, the faint stubble on his cheeks emphasising the hollows of his thin face, the expressive mouth softened and defenceless. For a moment vivid memories of their first meeting came back to her and she wanted to cover the still form with a blanket. Common sense stopped her. The last thing she should do was anything that might wake the sleeping tiger. With infinite care, she moved past him to the kitchen.

Minutes later she made her careful way back through the living-room, a hot mug in her hand. Something had disturbed him: he had flung one arm over his eyes as though to protect them from the dim light of the early morning, but he still seemed deeply asleep. She turned away.

He let her get as far as the door. 'You might have made one for me,' he complained in a voice which was slightly hoarse.

She stared at him. He had not moved but there was something which might have been the distant shadow of a wry smile touching the corner of his mouth. He was still shielding his eyes.

'If I move, my head will probably fall off,' he explained in a carefully controlled voice. 'Coffee might just help.'

He didn't *sound* angry. 'I'll get you some,' she agreed.

'Just don't clatter anything loudly,' he pleaded.

She brought two aspirins along with the coffee and discovered that he had managed to sit up, although he was holding his head in a way that told its own story. He looked up as she approached. The grey eyes were bloodshot, but the faint smile reappeared as he saw her holding out the cup and the tablets.

'Like old times, isn't it?' he said drily. No. After last night, nothing would be quite the same again, but she said nothing. He clasped the drink gratefully in both hands and she saw that he was shivering slightly, but decided it would be wiser not to comment. Despite his state, he must have sensed her uncertainty. He grimaced as he swallowed the aspirin, but said, 'Don't worry, I'm not going to tear you limb from limb. I'm not even going to shout at you.' He winced at the idea. 'All else apart, it would hurt *me* too much. Next time, though, remind me not to ask stupid questions at the wrong moment.'

Next time? There wasn't going to be one. 'I'm sorry——' she began, and was glad when he interrupted. She had no idea where that sentence might have been going.

'So am I,' he agreed, 'but I suppose I can't hold you entirely to blame for the hangover.' He carefully righted the fallen glass and screwed the top back on the bottle as though even the smell was upsetting him.

'Can I help?' she asked, uncertain what to do.

He looked at her. There wasn't as much humour as she had hoped in the dark-circled eyes. 'I don't think so. I suggest we avoid each other for the rest of this morning at least. *I*,' he stated positively, 'am going to finish this coffee, stagger upstairs, shower, shave, and then go to bed. Alone. If you're lucky I'll be nearly human by this afternoon.'

And meanwhile she could do anything she liked as long as she didn't come near him. That was obvious, and she supposed she couldn't blame him. She returned to her own room and quietly shut the door.

A few minutes later, she heard him come up the stairs. She felt no inclination to offer help. Interfering in Craig's life had got her here in the first place; it didn't seem a good moment to make matters worse.

Time dragged past. There was a limit to the number of hours she wanted to spend staring at pictures, however good. What she really wanted was to get out, walk for miles—and, preferably, not come back. On the dressing table, the heavy topaz lay ignored. She hadn't been able to bring herself to put it on this morning. She wasn't sure she ever wanted to wear it again. She looked around the comfortable room and thought regretfully of her own cramped studio flat. Right now its simplicity, and above all its privacy, held great appeal.

Why not? On his own admission, Craig would be out of action for the rest of the morning, and she could easily take a taxi.

She ran downstairs, made a quick phone call, and was waiting by the door when the taxi drew up. She had left Craig a note so he wouldn't worry in the unlikely event that he did notice her absence; she'd even told him when to expect her back.

When they arrived at the familiar shabby house she asked the driver to come back for her in two hours. Inside, the little room still smelled of fresh paint, but the air was stale. She flung open the window and then surveyed the single room. She'd made a good job of the decorating, she decided. The place was far more appealing than when she had first moved in. So where was the feeling of homecoming that she'd anticipated? She felt nothing.

Moodily, she wandered round the familiar, but somehow strange, surroundings. Now she was here it was hard to recall just why she'd made the impulsive decision to come. Even Sally was out. Still, she was stuck here for two hours; she might as well make herself comfortable.

Two hours later she had cleared out the fridge, a job she had forgotten in that first hurried departure, and packed a small plastic carrier with clothes she thought she might want. After that she spent half an hour sitting on the sofa-bed waiting for the taxi.

For most of the journey back, she found herself trying to suppress an irrational sense of anticipation. It was only as they drew up outside the house and she saw its door open as she got out of the car that doubts set in.

He didn't say anything as she passed him and went upstairs. He was clean-shaven and neat now, but she felt that she might have been better off with the dishevelled sufferer of the morning.

'Well?' she challenged as they entered the living-room. She had no intention of apologising for a perfectly reasonable excursion, but his expression was making her nervous so it was easier to be hostile. 'Is something wrong?'

'Not a lot,' he said, but his voice sounded strained as though he was gritting his teeth, and his hands were restrained by being thrust deep in his trouser pockets. 'If you decide to jaunt all over London, I suppose I've no way of stopping you. But it rather defeats the purpose of our arrangement.'

'But I took a taxi,' she protested, beginning to feel guilty. The taxi hadn't been Toby-approved. '*And* I left a note,' she added defensively.

'Which I found twenty minutes ago,' he said grimly. 'I spent the hour before that wondering whether you'd been mugged, murdered or kidnapped, and trying to decide where I should look first. It didn't,' he added with elaborate care, 'do much for my headache.'

That explained a lot. 'I'm sorry you were worried,' she apologised. 'I honestly didn't expect you to surface so quickly.' She didn't see what else she could say—that she'd assumed he would have passed out for the rest of the day?

'I wish I hadn't,' he muttered.

Exasperation overcame the shreds of remorse. 'Look,' she snapped, 'it wasn't my idea to come here in the first place and I'm beginning to think the whole charade is pointless anyway. We haven't heard a thing from your friends, *or* from your hypothetical terrorist, and I don't intend to stay a prisoner here indefinitely.'

He looked at her, and for a moment she thought he would annihilate her, then an indefinable air of defeat replaced the anger in his face. He shrugged. 'All right.

It's your life, I suppose, and I can't say I'm getting much fun out of being your nanny.' He spoke with utter indifference and turned away. She heard him walk downstairs, and then the studio door clicked shut.

It was as though he had slapped her. She had been ready for argument, not dismissal. Had he decided that it was, after all, just a fuss about nothing? Well, he'd given her tacit permission to do what she liked, and she had no intention of sitting around waiting for him to cool down. Without pausing to think about what she was doing, she ran downstairs and out of the front door into the autumn sunlight.

The streets were quiet and she had no particular destination in mind; she just wanted some fresh air. Unthinking, she found herself retracing the route she and Craig had taken days ago. In the park there were one or two people wandering idly: a mother pushing a pram, an old man with an equally elderly dog, a pair of lovers. She seemed to be the only one on her own.

She strolled along aimlessly, kicking at the scattering of leaves along the verges. The air was sweet and damp, a relief from the traffic fumes of the road. She supposed she ought to be trying to make some decisions about her future, but it was much easier to enjoy the unexpected pleasures of fresh air and solitude. Thinking was too likely to prove uncomfortable.

'*Jane!*' The shout behind her was furious.

She turned quickly to see Craig striding towards her with a dangerous expression on his face. He looks almost murderous, she thought, and glanced around, wondering wildly if the leafy bushes offered some hiding place.

What happened next made no real sense until long afterwards; she just acted without thought. Something was glinting in the rhododendrons, a figure crouching, holding something, half turned towards Craig. She suddenly knew that none of their fears had been groundless.

Terrified, she screamed, '*Craig!* Look out!' and began running towards the half-hidden figure who had swung round in her direction as she cried out.

The path was slippery with wet leaves and she stumbled, feeling sudden despair as she realised she could not reach the man before he pulled the trigger. She was falling, and a terrifyingly loud noise seemed to fill the air. There was a brief moment of pain, then darkness.

Somewhere a child was crying noisily. She wished its mother would take it away. She had a headache. But surely it was Craig who had the headache? Craig! Sudden fear, worse than any physical pain, made her cry out and open her eyes, wincing at the bright light. Above her, Craig's face swam into focus, a frown drawing his face into angry lines.

'I'm sorry——' she began.

His face cleared, his voice amazingly gentle. 'Don't be. You're a heroine. Don't try to move: we're waiting for an ambulance.'

An ambulance? Vaguely she remembered the noises. 'Did he shoot me?' she asked. Craig was holding her hands in a reassuring clasp; she didn't *feel* badly hurt. There was just this ache above her right eye.

He chuckled. 'No, he missed. You fell flat on your face at exactly the right time. You knocked yourself out, though, and I want the hospital to check you properly. You're going to have a lovely black eye,' he added unfeelingly.

'Thanks.'

She shut her eyes again. It didn't seem worth resenting his apparent good humour, not as long as he didn't let go of her hands.

He insisted on travelling to the hospital with her in the ambulance. When she refused a stretcher, declaring that she was perfectly capable of walking if someone would help her, he simply bent down and lifted her in his arms.

'Stop struggling, and just do as you're told for once,' he said. But he didn't sound angry and the arms which cradled her were gentle.

She realised, muzzily, that she didn't even *want* to struggle. Obediently, she looped her arms round his neck, leaning her aching head against the solid warmth of his shoulder.

The world swam dizzily again as more willing hands lifted her into the white van. There were people crowding round and she thought someone was asking her questions but Craig's imperious, 'You'll have to wait until later,' stopped them. That was fine. Craig could take care of everything. She shut her eyes and let the world drift a little further away.

She felt the jolting of the ambulance and heard the noise of their arrival at the hospital. This time it didn't seem worth protesting about the stretcher; she was feeling slightly sick. There was a confusing, blurred journey along an endless corridor then everything tilted and she was being lifted on to a bed.

'Craig?' she asked, surfacing briefly.

The hand that held hers tightened briefly and then let go. 'I'm here. I'll be waiting for you when you come back from X-ray.'

In fact it was the next morning when she learned from the nurses that he had indeed waited. She had by then been given 'something to make you sleep' and had been unaware of anything around her. He had apparently stayed until the doctors had confirmed that there was no serious damage, only leaving after he had been allowed in to see her and told that she would sleep for the rest of the day and the coming night.

'The poor man was worried sick about you. He kept asking the doctor if you were all right, even when he'd been told a dozen times that you'd be fine.' The nurse seemed to find it all very romantic. Craig hadn't seemed very worried to Jane when he had carried her into the ambulance, but perhaps she hadn't been in a suitable state to judge.

Evidently the doctor's reassurances had finally convinced him. He was not there to see her that morning. She was absurdly disappointed. She supposed she should have been glad to hear that he had at least phoned to check on her condition. When he had heard that she could be discharged that afternoon he had left a message to say that he would collect her at three.

By then, with only a faint headache and an enormous bruise to show for the previous day's adventure, Jane was more than ready to leave. Everyone had been very kind, but she found the hospital stifling and, besides, she was consumed with curiosity to discover exactly what *had* happened the day before. The interest and quickly suppressed speculation of the nursing staff did not help, nor did the fact that not even the closest reading of the papers offered any real information. The only reference to the incident was a comment that 'Miss Jane Simpson, fiancée of photographer Craig Stanton, has been taken to hospital after a fall. She is not seriously hurt.' She knew that: it was what was left unsaid that she wanted to discover, and Craig was her only source of information.

When he came to her room that afternoon, Jane could see no trace of the anxiety reported by her imaginative nurse. He surveyed her with detachment as she got up quickly from the chair by the bed. She thought his lips tightened slightly as he took in her appearance, but his tone was casually cheerful.

'I was right about the black eye,' he observed. 'It's not really your colour, is it?'

She already felt self-conscious about the darkening bruise; this made her glare at him, losing the faint sense of self-pity she had been feeling beneath a familiar exasperation.

'Next time I'll leave you to the thugs,' she snapped.

He grinned. 'Too late. The last thug has now been cornered, thanks to you.'

Despite her immediate demand for information, he refused to say anything else.

'Wait until we get home,' he told her, taking her arm as they walked down the echoing corridor.

Home? It sounded marvellous, but she'd better be careful about thinking of the Chelsea house as home. It was too easy.

Craig helped her into a taxi and, under strict instructions, the driver took them carefully and slowly back to the house.

'Go and sit down,' he instructed as they went upstairs together. 'I'll make some tea. Or do you want to go to bed?'

There was no double meaning, only concern in his voice, and she felt unexpected tears prick her eyes. She must be more tired than she realised.

'No, thanks,' she said firmly. 'I've had enough rest for the moment; I'm perfectly fit and I've no intention of going anywhere at all until I've heard every gory detail.'

'I might have guessed: as stubborn as ever,' he said, but he didn't sound annoyed. 'Actually, you were the most gory part of the proceedings. Let me get the tea and I'll give you a blow-by-blow account.'

All things considered, that was probably an accurate description of events. Jane leaned back against the chair's soft cushions, tucking her feet beneath her and shutting her eyes for just a moment. It was a relief to be sitting down again.

She opened her eyes to see Craig standing, watching her, looking both amused and exasperated. 'Not tired and perfectly fit?' he queried. 'Have some tea.'

She took the cup he was offering and decided not to try to defend her moment's lapse. 'I'll be fine by tomorrow,' she insisted.

'Of course,' he agreed.

'Well?' she demanded. 'What happened?'

His ready humour faded. 'You almost got yourself killed,' he told her bluntly. He sighed. 'It wasn't your fault—I lost my temper too, and the situation recently has been a bit oppressive.'

He could say that again. 'True,' she muttered. 'But why did the thug—whoever he was—suddenly appear like that when we haven't seen a trace of him before?' she wanted to know.

'Ah.' He hesitated. 'That's because of something you didn't really know about.'

Why should he expect that to surprise her? 'Go on, tell me what happened. *All* of it this time,' she added firmly.

'Fair enough. What you didn't realise, and what has kept our friend at a distance, was that neither of us went out of the house without someone—friends of Toby's— following us. Every time we went out, I'd made a call just beforehand to alert them. Our thug was obviously clever enough to spot them.'

'I see.' She remembered the chances she'd given him. 'So yesterday——' she began slowly.

'Yesterday,' he interrupted bitterly, 'I told you to get on with your own life—and almost ended it for you.'

'No!' she protested. 'You were angry, of course. But it wasn't your fault!'

He shrugged. 'That's a matter of opinion. The inescapable fact is that it resulted in your going out of the house before I'd realised what you might do, and you were almost at that wretched park before I'd managed to ring for reinforcements and come after you.'

No wonder he'd sounded so angry when he'd shouted. He must have been appalled by what she had done. 'But it was you he was aiming at,' she remembered with sick horror.

'He'd have taken either of us, even if I was his first choice. Anyway, you became the target the second you shouted that warning,' he added, his expression grim as he recalled that moment. 'If you hadn't fallen——' he began.

'But I did,' she reminded him. There was a white set to his lips, and she didn't want to relive those moments when she had been certain he was doomed. 'What I really want to know,' she went on, 'is what happened next.'

He relaxed slightly. 'Confusion. I thought you'd been shot, women were screaming, and our security guards came pounding up to trample the rhododendrons.'

'And?' she insisted.

'I didn't see it all,' he admitted. His tone was too casual; that must have been when he was checking that she was alive. 'But I gather it wasn't much of a fight in the end. The gunman never stood a chance of getting away and was marched off to the discreetly unmarked car by our rather shame-faced guardians. They send their apologies, by the way.'

'Why?' she objected. 'It was my fault, not theirs.'

'We can agree to differ about blame,' he told her drily. 'Anyway, I spent most of this morning discussing our friend's future with Toby—who sends you his thanks and compliments,' he added without much enthusiasm.

Yes, Toby would be grateful that her rash act had forced the pursuer into the open. Now that she was safe, she was quite relieved herself. And that also explained why Craig had not been at the hospital this morning. Jane felt curiously comforted and was suddenly overtaken by an enormous yawn. He was watching her.

'The doctor said you still needed to rest. You'd better go to bed when you've heard the end of the story.'

'Which is?' she asked, no longer quite so interested. Now that she was back here, warm and relaxed and the anger and danger all past, the drama of yesterday's events seemed almost unimportant. She stifled another yawn. Craig smiled.

'I'll make it brief. He turned out to be what we always suspected, an unofficial loner acting out of wounded pride. He was, as you thought, one of the lot who'd followed me to Athens. The others had apparently given it up once they realised they couldn't stop me handing over the film, but he decided to go it alone and at least get some revenge out of it. I suppose he might have been rewarded if he'd been successful. As it is, he's embarrassed his government and, since he had diplomatic immunity, is about to be shipped back home to make his excuses there. I don't think I envy him,' Craig finished thoughtfully.

'I don't care what happens to him—he deserves it all. At least we're safe now. Aren't we?' she added with a trace of anxiety because Craig was frowning.

His expression cleared. 'Absolutely. The guards are all withdrawn, the door's unbarred and the portcullis is up.'

'So it's all over?' She felt curiously flat. The implications of their safety were suddenly rather depressing. Tiredness washed over her.

He must have read something in her face. 'We'll talk about it in the morning. You look all in. I gather you've only been allowed out on condition you take things easy and get plenty of rest. Finish your tea, then you're going to bed.'

'Don't bully me.' It was a feeble protest and she knew it. She didn't even want to resist when he took the cup from her hand and pulled her to her feet.

'Upstairs,' he ordered. 'Can you walk, or shall I carry you?'

'I can walk,' she said with dignity. She'd need to feel a lot fitter than she did at the moment before she could cope with being swept off her feet by Craig. But he still insisted on going up with her and running her bath.

Slipping between crisp sheets twenty minutes later was an almost unbearable relief. Craig had drawn the curtains and the light in the room was dim. She shut her eyes, letting sleep wash over her.

She stirred once in the night, struggling briefly to the surface of consciousness from broken dreams of pursuit and fear. Vaguely, she felt there was someone in the room, watching her. It was oddly comforting and she smiled as she slipped back into calmer sleep.

She woke late next morning. That curious feeling of being observed had gone: a fugitive, pleasant dream. She stretched lazily; there were a few aches, but she was almost herself again. A tap on the door. That must have been what had woken her. She smiled. Just like the first morning.

Craig came in, carrying a tray which he put down on the table by the bed. His expression bore no resemblance to the cheerfulness of the first morning. Jane's sense of well-being began to ebb.

'Awake and feeling better?' he asked.

'Yes, to both.' She struggled to sit up. She had a feeling that any other answer would have wrecked whatever he was planning. There was a set look to his face which she did not understand, and which she did not like.

He stood looking down at her for a long moment, hands deep in his jeans pockets, before he spoke again. 'Do you feel up to talking about the future?' he asked at last, a sort of abruptness in his voice.

Despite the warmth of the bed, Jane felt chilled. She had hoped for at least a day's reprieve. Clearly she wasn't going to get it.

'Yes,' she agreed with a brightness that sounded false even to her own ears, although Craig didn't seem to notice it. 'We'd better get things sorted out, I suppose.'

'Good.' His reply was depressingly brisk. 'I'll see you downstairs when you feel like getting up. Don't hurry,' he added unconvincingly, leaving the room before she could do more than nod agreement. He obviously didn't want to stay around and chat. What had happened to all the teasing and concern?

Well, she wasn't going to stay around where she wasn't welcome. She dressed carefully, still feeling fragile, and went downstairs, bracing herself for whatever he might have to say. He looked up as she joined him in the living-room but stayed where he was, over by the window. With the light at his back, it was hard to tell what he was thinking, but his stillness wasn't encouraging. Perhaps she owed him a way out—and at least she might keep some shreds of her own dignity if she anticipated him.

'Go on, then: tell me the worst. Are you jilting me?' she demanded as cheerfully as she could. It hurt more badly than she had expected.

His answering smile was one-sided, but he didn't pretend to misunderstand. 'I think I ought to be a gentleman for once and do it the other way round. Don't you want to storm out of my life in disgust at my unspeakable behaviour, or something? The papers would love it. We can always say that your recent adventure was a chance encounter with a mugger following your walk-out after a row, if you like.'

She didn't like at all, even if it wasn't so very far from the truth. He had clearly worked it all out already. 'If the row was that spectacular, why am I here?' she objected, more because he seemed to expect some contribution from her than because she cared at all what the papers, or anyone else, thought. 'Shouldn't you have abandoned me in hospital?'

He seemed to be giving it serious thought. Jane was conscious only of a wish that she hadn't woken up that morning, or that this whole discussion could be over and done. 'I see what you mean,' he decided eventually, 'but we can hardly smuggle you back in and, anyway, while I don't mind being the villain of the piece, I do draw the line at casting you off while you're in hospital.'

'I'm the one doing the casting off,' she reminded him. It was all beginning to seem grotesquely unreal. Like planning her own funeral. She knew it was what they had always intended, but it was happening too easily. She had vaguely assumed that today would be marked by at least some sort of rejoicing and congratulations all round: this wasn't her idea of a celebration.

'So you are,' he was agreeing, obviously uninterested in anything but getting on with his interrupted life. 'Any suggestions?'

'You want me to leave today?' she asked. Why not? Staying around would evidently be inconvenient and embarrassing.

'The timing's entirely up to you.' She preferred Craig when he was being rude; this polite deference to her wishes made her feel like a stranger. 'You probably ought to have a few more days' rest before you do anything,' he offered.

For a moment, she was tempted. She could stay on here for a day or two—and then what? He would be civil and polite and she would be utterly miserable. No, he had done all that he had set himself to do; the debts were all paid. The least she could do was get out of his life with as little fuss as possible.

'No, I'm fine. Why don't I just go back to my flat? Inquisitive journalists aren't likely to find me there, and I don't even need to answer the phone if I don't want to.' The idea of being alone was suddenly powerfully attractive. Craig was frowning.

'I don't like the idea of your being on your own,' he said.

She did. 'Don't worry about it. Sally can keep an eye on me if it's necessary and the doctor said there was nothing wrong that a quiet day or two wouldn't put right. I'll be perfectly OK,' she insisted as he continued to look doubtful. Doctors didn't have any medicine for what was wrong with her, and staying here wasn't going to cure it either.

He clearly couldn't think of any other solution, and the mention of Sally seemed to reassure him slightly. 'If you're sure?' he began and she nodded, then wished she hadn't. She was getting a headache. 'I'll organise a taxi when you're ready, if you like,' he decided, clearly pleased that it was all so straightforward. 'Will you phone to confirm that Sally's in?'

'Fine.' Nothing was fine. She felt like something left over from her own funeral and Craig's eagerness to get rid of her, and the lack of all his usual humour, only made things worse. It was as though she had just become a loose end that needed tidying and all that they had shared had been an inconvenient interruption to his normal life. She didn't much want to contact Sally, but she would have to: Craig's conscience probably wouldn't let her arrive at the flat without someone to look after her.

It wasn't an easy phone call. Sally's first response was total disbelief.

'What do you mean, it's not going to work?' she demanded. 'I've never seen anything working better in my life!'

'Not any more,' Jane told her tiredly. 'Do you mind playing nursemaid for a day or two if I come home?' she repeated her original question.

Perhaps there had been something in her tone that told her friend she couldn't take much questioning, because Sally's voice softened. 'Of course not. Do you want me to come over and pick you up? Now?'

'No.' Conversation was getting difficult. 'Craig's organising that,' she explained, hearing her voice thickening. 'We're not exactly at each other's throats.' And a blazing row would be so much easier to cope with, she thought, but didn't say it. 'See you this afternoon,' she finished and put the phone down, aware of a hundred unasked questions at the other end.

She told Craig what she had organised and then decided to go and lie down. He was all concern for her headache, but she couldn't help wondering whether that was only in case she found herself unfit to leave.

She slept for a couple of hours and woke unrefreshed to pack and tidy up. It didn't take long and the lovely room soon lost all trace of her recent occupancy. Before she left she weighed the topaz ring in her hand for the last time. If she tried to give it back to Craig, he would tell her to keep it. She put in the dressing-table drawer; he would find it there eventually and could take it back to Sam for her. Picking up the folder of notes and photographs, she took one last look around the room and walked downstairs.

He was in the living-room, his back to her, staring out of the window. She must have made some sound as she came in because he swung round, his expression remote and unreadable.

'Ready?' he asked.

'I think so. What do you want to do about this?' She held up the folder.

He took it from her, dropping it dismissively on a table, not even glancing at it. 'Let's leave it for now. I expect you'll soon have plenty of work of your own to do. I'll go and get your case.'

Slowly, she walked downstairs and out to the waiting taxi. She didn't want to linger in the house. He would never contact her about the book. It had, after all, been only a device to keep her occupied.

CHAPTER TEN

THE journey back to the flat with Craig was silent: both interminable and too short. Once, he started on what had sounded as though it might have become thanks for her help; she cut him off sharply. She didn't want to remember that nightmare afternoon and, above all, she did not want Craig's gratitude. Eventually, it was easier to seem to doze, a dull headache pounding behind her eyes.

Once they arrived Sally was, for her, surprisingly tactful. She stayed with Jane and it was she who, in the awkward moment after Craig had put down the suitcase he had been carrying, said briskly, 'I'll see you out.' She had ushered him away, allowing neither of them a chance for more than the briefest, most formal of goodbyes.

It was several minutes later before Sally returned but Jane did not ask what she and Craig had found to talk about, nor did her friend volunteer the information. She remained long enough to help make up the bed and offer to stock the fridge next day but it was only as they finished unpacking that she said to Jane, who had hardly spoken since her arrival, 'Do you want to talk about it?'

Dumbly, Jane shook her head. 'Not yet,' she managed. Perhaps never.

Sally hugged her, and left. 'We'll have a party in a day or two—when your headache's gone,' she promised. A reluctant smile tugged at Jane's lips. Was Sally running short of food?

When she was left alone, the momentary amusement faded fast. Jane looked around the small room. This was all she had now; she would just have to pull herself together and get on with her life. Tomorrow. She sat on the newly made bed and closed her eyes against the sharp sting of involuntary tears.

The long, empty hours of the next few days crept aimlessly past and she seemed to exist in a kind of fog, unable to settle to anything. She couldn't even find the energy to phone her mother and tell her of the changed situation. It would have to be done soon, she supposed without much interest. Her apathy eventually began to worry Sally, who feared that the head injury might have been worse than Jane had admitted. She insisted on bringing in a doctor. It didn't take his comments to reassure Jane; she knew that what she was suffering from had no physical cause. It was a pity that it didn't seem likely to fade as fast as the yellowing marks on her face.

At last she decided she just had to make an effort, if only to go for a walk. If her feet led her to Bond Street and left her stranded outside Craig's exhibition, should she have been surprised? She looked at the poster in the window and the indications that the show was as popular as ever as people came and went, talking eagerly about what they had seen. She couldn't just loiter in the street indefinitely, but somehow it was hard to move away. Then she remembered Craig recommending that she have a second look at the pictures when she was more used to the idea. Perhaps she should. Perhaps she could see what he had found to interest him in her less than glamorous appearance. Hesitantly, she opened the door.

The man at the reception desk looked up, but didn't really see her. 'Yes?' he asked. Then he frowned. 'Aren't you——?' he began.

'I am,' she agreed wearily.

'This is marvellous,' he said with unwelcome enthusiasm. 'I'll tell Mr. Stanton you're here.'

'No!' It was the last thing she wanted. She hadn't thought Craig might be around—or had she? No, they would both be far too embarrassed by any encounter here. She must leave. 'No,' she repeated more calmly, seeing the young man's astonished expression. 'I'm not staying after all; please don't bother him.' She had left the building before his half-formed questions could take shape, or before she could glimpse a familiar sardonic smile, or the quizzical tilt of that brown-blond head, across the room.

It had been a mistake coming here, but even as she walked away she found her steps lagging. Walking away was harder the second time. Other people were emerging behind her, talking earnestly. Despite the last encounter, she couldn't resist slowing to overhear. Just to hear someone praising Craig would somehow be satisfying.

'The Middle Eastern ones made me want to cry,' the girl was saying. 'How does he say so much without words?' Jane didn't know, but she knew what the girl meant.

'I liked the portraits,' her companion preferred. 'That girl's got something special.' No, she hasn't, Jane thought. And she threw away what she might have had. It was Craig who was special. Eavesdropping wasn't a good idea after all. Jane turned blindly away. She wanted to be at home.

She had bumped into the portly, upright figure before she saw him. She looked up through blurred eyes, muttered apologies beginning almost automatically. But he stopped her.

'Jane! How delightful to see you. I was going to drop in on Craig, but you'll do even better. Come and have some tea.'

Toby had turned her round and tucked her arm under his and begun walking her briskly away before she had time even to consider a protest.

He escorted her to the restaurant of a large hotel and had sat her down and ordered tea with fussy precision before allowing her to say anything beyond polite greetings. 'Congratulations and thanks for giving us the chance to let us tie up all the loose ends from that messy affair of Craig's,' he boomed briskly. 'And how are you and the boy getting on now that all the fuss is over?' he demanded as he spread the white napkin over his ample lap.

She blinked. Hadn't Craig told him? 'We aren't,' she said simply. 'I mean, the charade's all over now so I'm back in my own flat.'

He gestured for her to pour the tea. 'You are? He didn't tell me you were leaving.' He sounded disappointed. 'I thought he had more sense than that,' he added, half to himself.

Jane ignored that. 'There wasn't much point in staying on,' she said firmly. And then, because she couldn't help it, added, 'Is he going to go on doing crazy things for you?' she asked.

He shrugged, the pale blue eyes regarding her with that unexpected shrewdness. 'That depends on how much he wants to go on taking risks. Sometimes lately I've thought he was getting a trifle tired of it.' His glance lingered on her, seeming to read her concern and he came to a decision. 'He started when he was at university. I sometimes think I saw more of him than his father and, when he was killed, Craig suddenly had too many opportunities and not much direction. He had plenty of money, of course, but he didn't seem to give a damn about anybody or anything. Not that I blame him: anyone with his background could have turned out a lot worse.'

'I know,' Jane agreed softly. 'He told me a bit about it.'

Toby's bushy brows rose. 'Did he? That's unusual. Well, at least you can see why he might have enjoyed a bit of adventure from time to time—and it kept him from other sorts of trouble.'

Yes, she could understand that; a man with too much money and no ties or affections could take the wrong direction quite easily. Some of her resentment of Toby eased. He was still talking. 'I hoped he'd settle down once the photography started to be such a success, but he still got restless from time to time and wanted some excitement in his life.'

'What about Jillian?'

Toby's snort was expressive. 'Jillian? What about her? Women like her know exactly what they want from a man like Craig—and they certainly aren't interested in any problems he might have.'

'So what makes you think I am?' Jane challenged.

'Aren't you?'

She wasn't going to answer that. 'He's probably deeply relieved that all this fuss is over,' she said instead, 'and that he's rid of me.'

Toby appeared to consider this. 'I'm not so sure. In fact I was surprised when he agreed to the plan in the first place—whatever you might think of Jillian, he's never let anyone move in with him before.'

'The circumstances,' she reminded him drily, 'were rather different. Anyway, you didn't give him much choice.'

'That's never stopped him going his own way in the past,' Toby said, as though remembering a previous confrontation.

'He thought he owed me something,' Jane admitted. From the way Toby's frown cleared, he had evidently come across this element in Craig's character before. At any rate, he seemed to take it as an adequate explanation.

'I see,' he said with what might have been almost a trace of regret. 'But he's still been in a pretty odd mood since the attack on you. Worse tempered than usual. I did suggest an overseas trip and he almost bit my head off.' If it hadn't been so unlikely, Jane would have thought he sounded almost pleased. 'Have another cake,' he offered before she could make any comment.

He didn't seem to want to talk about Craig any more, and he'd given her enough to think about. Eventually, she glanced at her watch.

'I must go,' she decided, getting to her feet. 'Thanks for tea.'

'It's been a pleasure,' he said formally, and escorted her to the door before bidding her farewell.

On the walk back to the flat she concluded that the afternoon had not been a success. It had only made her think more about Craig than ever. It would be a mistake to go and sit and brood on her own for the evening; she would call on Sally.

They chatted about nothing that seemed very important for a while, the conversation flowing past Jane without making any real impression. Eventually Sally gave up. She tilted her head on one side, bright eyes regarding her friend curiously. 'Are you going to tell me what's wrong?' she demanded.

'Nothing time won't put right.' Jane didn't even convince herself.

'Nothing? When you've spent days in total apathy? The Jane I first met would have been all for tearing Craig limb from limb, or else laughing at her own idiocy. Sitting staring broodingly into space is just not like you. And you seem to have given up eating, too. Don't think I haven't noticed; you must have lost half a stone.'

She attempted an unconvincing smile. 'At least that's one good thing.'

'Nonsense. You look awful,' Sally told her candidly.

'Thanks. You're really cheering me up,' Jane muttered.

'No, I'm not, and I can't if I don't know what's wrong. Are you still in love with him?'

The flat question, on top of everything that had happened that day, was too much. She couldn't stop the flood of sudden, idiotic tears. Horrified, Sally crouched beside her, trying to make soothing noises.

Eventually, Jane sniffed, mopping her eyes with the large handkerchief, which smelled vaguely of turpentine, that was pushed into her hands. It probably doubled as a paint rag, she realised. At least the burst of tears had done some good; it seemed to have helped her come to a decision.

'I'm sorry about that,' she apologised, 'but if you want to hear the whole, dreary story, then I'd like to tell someone.'

Sally sat down. 'I want to hear it,' she said firmly. 'It's not as straightforward as you've been pretending, is it?'

Jane sniffed again, a faint smile, the first in days, touching her lips. 'It's not straightforward at all.'

She told Sally all about the whole absurd affair, going over the meeting on the ferry and the crazy photography session in Athens again, and then on to the melodrama of the final scene in the park. Her friend sat, fascinated and almost disbelieving, through the long tale, shock and curiosity chasing each other across her face.

'So you see,' Jane finished, 'there was no reason at all to continue the engagement once the thug had been dispatched home again. That's why it's all over.'

Sally wasn't a fool. 'If it was a pretence there'd be no problem, would there?' she said quietly. 'It's not over, is it?'

Jane sighed. 'Oh, I'll get over him eventually, I expect. It's not his fault that I've made the same mistake as every other besotted female around. At least he doesn't know how I feel—I have my pride.' Her laugh was meaningless and Sally didn't join in. She was looking serious, almost, Jane thought, disapproving.

'I know it's not the sort of thing I'm meant to ask, and you can always tell me to mind my own business,' she said bluntly, 'but were you lovers?'

Jane flushed. 'No,' she admitted, 'although even now I'm not sure if I'm glad or sorry about it.' She hadn't tried to hide the feeling between Craig and herself. 'I suppose you're going to congratulate me on having escaped without too much damage,' she added wearily.

Sally's response shocked her. 'I'm not going to do anything of the sort,' she said in a voice that had lost a lot of its sympathy. 'Let's get this straight: am I right in thinking that you love Craig?'

That was the heart of it. 'I think so. I don't know.' She had wanted love to be a calmer, more certain emotion, not this whirlpool. If this *was* love, it frightened her. How could something so intense last?

'And I take it you haven't mentioned it to him because he made it plain he's not the marrying kind and you wanted to salvage that pride you mentioned?' There was definite impatience in Sally's voice now.

'I suppose so,' Jane agreed cautiously. Put like that, it didn't sound very pleasant.

'Well, if you want my opinion—and I don't suppose you do—I think you've been a fool,' Sally told her flatly.

Jane was taken aback. She hadn't wanted to be smothered in sympathy, but she hadn't expected attack either. She was willing to agree about her folly, but she had a feeling Sally's viewpoint was different from her own.

'In what way?' she wondered cautiously.

'Almost every possible way, probably, including interfering right at the start,' added Sally in a softer tone. 'Mind you, I can see the temptation,' she admitted with a distinctly wicked grin. Then she went on more seriously, 'Pride has never been one of the vices I admired; it usually ends up hurting its owner. And, whatever your Craig may think, love—or even desire—shouldn't automatically demand a return. However pleasant it may be if it gets one. I know you said he was the one who was frightened of commitment, but what about you? Haven't you been holding back a bit?'

She hadn't looked at it that way before. 'I was afraid——' she began, remembering all her doubts about love's permanence.

'Isn't everyone? But you've got yourself hurt anyway, haven't you? What happened to the girl who was fed up with playing it safe and decided to take a few chances? I went to that exhibition, too, you know. When I saw those photos of you,' she went on slowly, 'I couldn't help thinking how well he'd seen you. He'd caught all that bubbly life that makes everyone else feel alive.' Sally grinned: Jane didn't recognise the portrait of herself in her friend's words. 'Now I'm not so sure,' her friend finished.

Jane stared at her. Sally was making her see recent events in a way that had never occurred to her, and they didn't make her feel any more comfortable.

Before she could comment, Sally went on, 'Are you sure he doesn't care for you at all? He certainly sounded worried enough when you came back here; he left me with an impressive list of instructions in case you started to feel ill again. I'd say he's been pretty protective—and you certainly can't say he's taken advantage of you.'

The old-fashioned phrase sounded so incongruous from Sally that it gave Jane a moment of amusement. It was about the only comfort she could find among thoughts that were in confusion. The fog of gloom she had been hugging to herself had been torn mercilessly away and she didn't like what she was forced to see. She looked up to meet the concern in her friend's eyes.

Yes, Craig had been protecting her from the thugs. But that wasn't what Sally had meant. 'You're right,' she admitted at last. 'I might have saved him from a bruise or two; he's kept saving me from myself.' She remembered his restraint, his concern, the consideration he'd shown. He'd teased her about the chemistry, but he'd never forced the issue. And he'd known she wouldn't have put up much of a fight. 'I never saw it,' she realised slowly. 'I just assumed he was protecting himself.'

Sally laughed. 'Don't assume he wasn't doing that, too. The man's been a loner for a long time now.' She hesitated. 'I'm sorry if I've upset you.'

Jane interrupted her. 'Don't be. Anyway, you haven't—or not as badly as I probably deserve. To think I used to despise people who wallowed in self-pity,' she mocked herself.

'Well, at least you've pulled out of it now. Perhaps I should drop in at Chelsea—just in case he needs comforting,' she teased.

Jane mimed a threatening snarl. 'Join the queue. I'm not as "out of it" as you might think. If Craig needs comfort, *I* intend to provide it. Besides,' she added with suddenly revived energy, 'he saved my life in the park. Sort of. This time *I* owe him.' It wasn't convincing, but any ammunition was better than none. What she was planning to do needed all the courage she could muster. 'If it all goes wrong, you can pick up the pieces,' she told Sally. 'He may throw me out on my ear, but nothing,' she said with real feeling, 'can be as bad as the past few days have been.'

Sally was laughing. 'I feel as though I've created a monster. Good luck, though. Do you want some Dutch courage first?' She gestured towards a bottle.

Jane was smiling as she went up to her own room. She'd declined the drink, but she still felt that absurd sense of relief and confidence. Upstairs, she felt anticipation, but no hurry. She took her time showering and trying to restore some order to her hair which she had allowed to become limp and unkempt. It dried back into bouncy life as though reflecting her own resurgence of energy. She contemplated herself in the mirror: Sally had been right. She had lost weight, possibly too much. Too bad; there wasn't much she could about that tonight.

It wasn't easy to decide what to wear. She didn't want to seem too festive, in case everything went humiliatingly wrong. Anything formal would be wrong, too. Eventually, realising she could dither for hours, she picked out an amber silk shirt and teamed it with her jeans and a patterned waistcoat. Over her coat she draped the soft shawl she hadn't been able to resist taking with her when she had left Craig's house.

It was dark by the time she set out. In the taxi, her sense of anticipation began to fade and nervousness set in as she realised what she was about to do. Beside it, all the other risks she had taken recently paled into insignificance. He was probably going to slam the door in her face. If he was in. If he didn't have a girlfriend with him. She almost told the driver to take her back to the flat, but then she remembered Sally's words and knew that anything would be better than returning to the apathy of the past week.

She left the taxi at the end of the road and walked alone up the quiet mews. At least there was a light on upstairs: he was in. She rang the bell and stood on the step wondering whether she had been mad to come. She wanted to run. And then Craig opened the door.

The light was on in the hall behind him and she couldn't see his face, but he went very still when he saw her.

'Hello,' she said stupidly.

'Hello,' he answered, not moving aside. Her eyes were adjusting to the light now. He looked dishevelled and again she feared there might be a woman waiting upstairs for him. Not Jillian. She couldn't bear that. He obviously found her silence irritating. 'What do you want?' he asked abruptly. 'I don't need a nursemaid any more. Remember?'

'I remember,' she said quietly, refusing to let his harshness deter her now. 'I also remember something else.'

'What?' His impatience was growing.

Now or never. She didn't know how to begin. But she had to. She clenched her hands in her coat pockets, looking anywhere but at him. 'I remember a chemical reaction and your opinion that it wouldn't go back in the cupboard.' She looked up, defenceless. 'You were right.'

He stared at her in silence and for a moment she wondered whether he'd understood. 'Are you saying what I think you are?' he demanded at last.

Her mouth was dry. 'Yes,' she said simply. 'Can I come in?'

His laugh was shaken, but there was a hint of real humour in his voice when he spoke. 'I think you'd better. The doorstep is definitely not the place to take this conversation any further.' He stepped back.

She went in and up the stairs to the familiar room. All the bright certainty of a few hours ago had gone, but at least he hadn't slammed the door in her face. And he was alone. Slipping off her coat and dropping it on a chair, she turned towards him. In the light of the living-room she was shocked to see his thin face drawn in lines of tiredness.

'You look ill!' she exclaimed.

'Thanks.' His voice was expressionless. 'I haven't been sleeping well,' he added. Hope began to grow again. A one-sided smile touched the fine planes of his face, but he kept his hands in his pockets and didn't approach her. 'Don't change the subject,' he told her quietly. 'You were going to tell me all about chemistry.'

'I wasn't... I mean, I don't know...' she began helplessly. How on earth did she *say* it?

And then there was no need to. He reached out a slightly unsteady hand to trace the lines of her jaw. She shivered. 'No last-minute retreat this time?' he asked seriously.

'None.' For the first time, she spoke with absolute certainty.

For a moment longer he held back, as though he still doubted her, so it was she who stepped forward into his arms, lifting her hands to his shoulders in surrender. Whatever happened in the future, *this* she knew was right: commitment didn't ask for guarantees. 'I'm here for as long as you want me,' she said simply, and lifted her face to his.

She was almost crushed by the strength of the arms that tightened round her. Then one hand was in her hair, tilting her head for his seeking mouth to explore her eyes, her cheeks and, finally, her lips. At first he ravished her mouth as though desperate to make up for the empty days, then, when she responded with all the strength of her own pent-up emotions, his lips gentled. He sampled all the sweetness that she offered with a lingering pleasure that set her pulse thudding. When at last he lifted his head, she tightened her arms around his neck, mutely protesting.

He looked down at her, grey eyes alive and sparkling with familiar mischief, 'It's all right,' he reassured her, 'it's just that I have no intention of trying to make love to you on that sofa. It's jinxed,' he remembered with feeling. 'Come upstairs,' he said softly.

For only the second time, she entered his room. Something seemed different about it, but the light was dim and all her senses were focused on Craig, who had drawn her back into his arms.

With all doubts and reservation cast aside, the fire that twice before had nearly consumed her was irresistible. She felt his fingers moving on the buttons of her blouse, their soft brush against her skin almost unbearably tantalising. Her own hands were no less busy against the soft cotton of his shirt. Then the silk was slipping from her shoulders and his hands were at her waistband.

They had both waited too long, were too impatient, to linger long on the delights of anticipation. Naked together on his bed, they touched as though needing convincing of each other's reality. Jane traced the long line of his body, the dip of his waist, the lean strength of his flanks. Then he took her hands, pinning them beside her head as his lips explored her, teasing and suckling her breasts, enjoying her uncontrolled response. Flames seemed to leap within her and her body arched towards his in final surrender.

'Please, Craig,' she whispered, moaning as his lips moved against her and she felt the heat of his body.

He lifted his head, looking down at her, helpless beneath him. For a moment she saw a gleam of almost savage triumph in his grey eyes before he moved over her willing body, completing and fulfilling her beyond her dreams.

Whatever he might have intended, it was no act of male dominance. Together, they both lost all control, passion driving them to a release past all imagining. For Jane, the only reality was the heat of Craig's back beneath her tightening hands and the surging force which united them. She felt a moment of giddy fear at her helplessness and then heard Craig cry out her name and knew that he was with her as she lost all capacity for coherent thought in the wave which engulfed them.

Minutes passed in a daze which was not far from unconsciousness. She could hear the rapid thud of Craig's heart, knew her own was pounding as hard, and felt it only slowly resume its normal rhythm. With an effort that was almost too great, she raised her head far enough to kiss his shoulder. He opened one eye and returned the caress, brushing his lips against the swell of her breasts, still tender from his earlier passion. Jane smiled lazily and let herself drift into a sort of half-sleep.

She felt Craig move away from her and muttered a protest. 'Don't go.'

His weight settled beside her, one arm around her shoulders drawing her against him so that her head was pillowed against his chest. She couldn't remember feeling so comfortable, so safe, before. She heard the rumble of his amusement. 'I'm not going anywhere. Even if I had the strength.'

Eventually the euphoria began to fade. Still cradled in his arms, she felt the cold breath of reality. They had made love and it had been an experience beyond any idea she had had of pleasure, or desire. Sally had been right: she had had to take a chance, but now she had so much more to lose that she didn't know how she was going to bear it.

Alert as ever to her emotions, he must have sensed her sudden doubts. He tilted her chin with one finger so that she had to meet his gaze, her own wide and vulnerable. 'What's wrong?'

It was too late to try to rebuild her defences. 'What happens next?' she wondered aloud, and felt the quiet laughter of his response.

'Give me ten minutes and I'll show you.' Then he went on in the same deceptive tone, 'After that, and if we have the strength, we might do something really shocking and get married. If, of course, we can bring ourselves to get up long enough to find a register office.'

She twisted from under his arm as he spoke, staring down at him in disbelief. 'What?' she demanded.

He pulled her down against him again. 'You heard.'

'But why?' It wasn't a gracious response to what was presumably a sort of proposal, but she didn't understand. 'You said——'

'I know what I said,' he interrupted, 'but even I can be wrong.' He stroked her hair gently. 'I didn't bargain on falling in love with you,' he explained simply.

It was too simple. Too impossible. 'Are you sure?' How could he be, when she was so suddenly full of doubts, frightened to trust this feeling that overwhelmed her? 'What is love?' she said softly, almost to herself.

The fingers on her hair stilled and he turned to drop a light kiss on her forehead. 'Laughing when you laugh?' he suggested, smiling with all the confidence she seemed to have lost. Then, more seriously, 'And hurting when you hurt; wanting to protect you; hating myself for endangering you; thinking of you almost constantly; aching for you in a way I never knew was possible. Shall I go on?'

'Sounds painful.' The flippant words were belied by the tears that choked her voice and tightened her throat.

'It is,' he agreed with feeling. 'It might be better, of course, if you reciprocated,' he added and, lying close against his naked body, she felt the tension behind the casual tone.

'More bargain hunting? More sale and exchange?' she wondered sadly, remembering their conversation in the taxi the day that they became engaged. She was almost afraid to believe what he seemed to be saying.

His hold on her tightened. 'Unfortunately not. Not any more.' His words wondered at his previous assurance. 'It seems to be a total commitment—whatever you feel.' There was an unspoken question there.

She hesitated. She hadn't thought this far ahead, hadn't believed it was possible. Now the doubts crept in. 'I don't know,' she admitted. 'I've never felt like this before. Perhaps it's just physical?'

His laugh was short and incredulous. '*Just?* If you say you've ever experienced anything like what we've just shared, I won't believe you. I know I haven't. Anyway,' he added acutely, 'you know you'd have been able to walk away if that was all it was.' He was right. His perception was almost too good, but his arms held her as though she was something infinitely precious, and her confidence began to return. 'What is it?' he asked quietly. 'You've never hesitated to take chances before.'

'I don't think I ever realised before what I might lose if I lost you,' she admitted, feeling as though her heart, as well as her body, was naked before him.

'Everything?' he asked softly, and pulled her close against him. She nodded mutely against the safe wall of his chest. He must have felt the movement because he went on, his lips brushing her hair, 'There aren't any guarantees, love. All I can say is that it's the same for me. Perhaps that counts for something?'

She eased herself away so that she could look at him. There was no doubt, no disguise in the gaze that met hers. 'I think it probably counts for everything,' she admitted, reaching up to kiss him. Their embrace was total commitment, all restraint gone between them.

'Do you know,' she said minutes later when their emotions had calmed a little, 'I think that the chemistry, as you called it, was one of our problems. I know I was too frightened of it ever to relax completely with you. It hid some of the other things we shared.'

'Like obstinacy?' he suggested.

'And a sense of humour,' she pointed out.

'That's true,' he agreed. 'I never seemed to have to explain a joke to you, or worry that you'd misinterpret some flippant comment. Though I was a bit startled when you wasted your drink on Jillian,' he teased. 'It also gave me some hope,' he added more seriously.

She remembered the remark that had sparked that incident. 'I wasn't quite myself,' she admitted, and saw his grin as she refused to mention the jealousy that had clawed at her. 'I suppose we were too busy fighting off the lust to notice how much liking there was under it,' she went on, following her original idea.

He chuckled. 'Something like that. But I wasn't trying to fight it off.'

'I noticed,' she said drily.

He ran the tip of one finger down the centre of her body, watching with interest the reaction she couldn't conceal. 'Are you still fighting?' he asked.

'No,' she told him, suddenly breathless.

Their lovemaking this time was all tenderness, with none of the desperate need of that first encounter. Craig seemed determined to find new ways to please her and she delighted in discovering the responsiveness of his body. For all their teasing and laughter, though, the end was as breathtaking as before.

This time they drifted into sleep afterwards, no longer either doubting or fearing the future.

Jane awoke to find the room still dark, but she sensed that Craig was watching her. She reached up to touch his face and felt his smile as he turned his head to kiss her fingers.

'Hello,' she said sleepily.

'Hello, yourself,' he responded. 'I didn't mean to wake you and I know it's very unromantic, but I'm afraid I'm starving. With one thing and another, I don't seem to have had much appetite lately,' he added ruefully.

She laughed, admitting, 'I know exactly what you mean.' She struggled upright against the pillows. 'Now you mention it, food doesn't sound like a bad idea.'

He got out of bed. 'Stay there. I'll go and find some sandwiches and champagne or something. Don't go away.' He kissed her quickly and left the room.

Left alone, Jane reached out and switched on the lamp. No wonder she'd thought the room looked different. She swung her feet to the floor and stood up, slipping on his discarded shirt against the cool air.

It was still a largely empty room, but that alarming bareness had gone. Apart from the scattering of clothes which she picked up with a reminiscent smile, there was a clutter of oddments on the chest, a small, surprising bowl of autumn crocuses on the table—and two pictures on the walls.

She didn't have to go and study them. They were the two photographs he had taken on the ferry. She heard the door open and turned. 'When did you put those up?' she asked.

He shut the door behind him and, putting down a tray, came to stand beside her. 'The day you left,' he admitted. She was bewildered and must have shown it because he pulled her back towards the bed, saying, 'Get under the covers and keep warm; I'll explain. But first...' He reached over for something on the tray and, lifting her left hand, slid the topaz back on to the ring finger. 'That stays there this time. OK?' She nodded, looking down at the glowing stone, finding it hard to speak. Craig grinned. 'I think I must have subconsciously already given in when I took you to Sam to get it.'

Had he? It had puzzled her then that he had taken her to an old friend—had he already been fighting himself, and not known it? She remembered the way he had recognised, as she had done, how perfect the ring was. Now she closed her hand on it, the charade that had become, against all the odds, a reality more precious than any gem.

'Good,' she said, her voice not quite steady. She stared down at the ring, at last beginning to believe in it, for a long moment before remembering the mystery he'd promised to explain. 'About the pictures...?' she prompted.

He poured champagne into two glasses, passing her one and touching his softly against it in silent toast. 'Yes. Well, even when it seemed unlikely I would see you again, I was too fascinated by you for my own good. Then Toby came up with his bright idea and I realised that if you were staying here there was a good chance that something—such as curiosity—would bring you in here.' She saw him smile as she coloured. 'So, since I didn't want you to get the wrong—or right—idea, and I'd already taken down the pictures I used to have up, I decided to leave the room as neutral as possible. A bit childish, I suppose,' he acknowledged as she listened, fascinated, 'but there was something about you that made me feel uncomfortably vulnerable even then.'

'It may have been childish, but it was very effective.' Jane remembered her first reaction to the stark room. 'And I know how you felt,' she admitted, recalling her own sense of vulnerability where he was concerned. It was difficult, but comforting, to realise that his control had been as fragile as her own.

His arm settled round her shoulders, his hands lingering against the smoothness of her skin as though touching something rare. 'I think I was doomed from the night we met,' he said with no apparent regret. 'I can't think why else I let you fuss over me on that ferry,' he teased. 'Then I was unreasonably pleased when I realised I'd have to come to Athens. It was the only excuse I needed to look you up. I thought everything was safe by then: nothing to worry about except whether you could possibly be as infuriating as you seemed.' A hard kiss interrupted her instinctive protest and she relaxed against him, smiling. 'Then the thugs reappeared—and you were right in the middle of things.' He sounded grim now and she remembered the brutal way he had tried to get rid of her. It had worked, too.

'I didn't think I'd see you again,' she admitted.

'You weren't going to. Then that letter arrived and I was absurdly glad to realise it meant I had to contact you. Then Toby dropped his bombshell.'

'I met him yesterday,' Jane recalled. It seemed an age ago: it was hard to remember how desperate things had felt then. 'He seemed almost disappointed to hear I'd moved out.'

Craig chuckled. 'I like the idea of Toby as Cupid,' he decided. 'I think I'll have to ask him to be my best man.'

'Will you still be working for him?' Jane asked with sudden anxiety. Craig wasn't someone you could tie down, but she wasn't sure she could cope with knowing he was in danger somewhere.

His response was reassuring. 'The only adventures I intend to indulge in from now on will involve you. You won't mind travelling with me, will you?'

'You couldn't leave me behind. Haven't I already proved my tenacity?' she reminded him. He laughed, but she had thought of something else. 'Do I get to help with the book again?' she wondered.

'You've no choice—we start work again tomorrow.' She nestled closer. 'Or possibly the day after. In fact I was going to use the book to lure you back if my nerve failed and I found I couldn't cope without you. I might have lasted a couple more days,' he said thoughtfully.

'Why *did* you get rid of me so fast?' she asked. If he had known then that he loved her, it seemed a strange thing to have done.

'Guilt, I think,' he answered soberly. 'I thought you were dead after that shot, you know.' His arm tightened and Jane saw the chill bleakness of remembered horror in his eyes and knew how she would have felt—*had* felt when she saw that gun pointing at him. 'Then I discovered you were alive and, although the danger was over, I felt as though I had brought you nothing but trouble. I planned to make sure you were fully recovered, then let you go.'

'So what went wrong?' She'd certainly not been recovered when she'd left.

He smiled ruefully. 'I discovered I couldn't trust myself. Even with you concussed and sporting a black eye...' he reached out to touch the fading bruise with fingers delicate as feathers '...I was horrified to discover that all I wanted to do was to get you into my bed as soon as possible. And keep you there. Even when you were asleep, I couldn't leave you.'

She remembered the half-waking dream. He sounded so remorseful that she had to turn and kiss him softly.

'I'm sorry I took so long to come to my senses,' she told him gravely. 'I think it was myself as much as you that I kept fighting: I didn't think love was like that. And I do love you, you know.'

She had thought it would be difficult to say, but somehow it was the most natural thing in the world. All the doubts that had haunted her were gone, swept away by a certainty as absolute as his. He reached out and took her glass and plate from her and drew her into his arms, not kissing her at first, just holding her.

As joy welled up in her, she began to feather small, delicate kisses along his shoulder. She felt him laugh. 'Optimist! Do your worst, woman.'

She needed no encouragement and, a very few minutes later, it was evident that he had misjudged his own stamina. His embrace on her was tightening as the telephone began to ring.

Holding her gaze with his, he reached out to pick up the instrument. Lying on top of him, she expected him to blast the caller and then return to her; instead she saw his eyebrows lift and felt the beginning of suppressed laughter. Wordlessly, he lifted the receiver towards her ear.

'Jane? Is that you?' demanded the familiar voice. 'I thought you were going to call me this week?'

'I'm sorry, Mother,' she managed. 'I've been a bit busy.'

'Does that mean you've got the wedding arrangements started at last?'

Jane glanced down at Craig who was listening while with one hand he stroked the curve of her back. 'Something like that,' she agreed, smiling softly.

Craig took the receiver from her. 'Hello, it's Craig here,' he said. 'I think you and the rest of the family had better catch the first plane over. We've decided not to wait. Haven't we?' he added in a quiet aside to Jane who nodded vigorously and retrieved the phone.

'Mother, it'll be lovely to see you and everyone else, but can you please wait until we're all in the same time-zone before you call again? Love to Ben,' she added and replaced the instrument firmly while Craig removed the plug from its socket.

'Now,' he said, laughter dancing in his eyes, 'where were we?'

Next month's Romances

Each month, you can choose from a world of variety in romance with Mills & Boon. These are the new titles to look out for next month.

A FIERY BAPTISM Lynne Graham
A TIME TO DREAM Penny Jordan
SLEEPING PARTNERS Charlotte Lamb
RUNAWAY FROM LOVE Jessica Steele
DARK CAPTOR Lindsay Armstrong
DARK AND DANGEROUS Mary Lyons
AN UNFINISHED AFFAIR Jenny Arden
THE GYPSY'S BRIDE Rosalie Ash
ISLAND INTERLUDE Anne McAllister
RIDE A STORM Quinn Wilder
AN EARLY ENCHANTMENT Stephanie Wyatt
A MATTER OF HONOUR Stephanie Howard
LOVE'S DOUBLE FOOL Alison York
RIGHT CONCLUSIONS Helena Dawson
ICE LADY Emma Goldrick

STARSIGN
ON GOSSAMER WINGS Shirley Kemp

Available from Boots, Martins, John Menzies, W.H. Smith, Woolworths and other paperback stockists.

Also available from Mills and Boon Reader Service, P.O. Box 236, Thornton Road, Croydon, Surrey CR9 3RU.

While away the lazy days of late Summer with our new gift selection
Intimate Moments

Four Romances, new in paperback, from four favourite authors.
The perfect treat!

The Colour of the Sea
Rosemary Hammond

Had We Never Loved
Jeneth Murrey

The Heron Quest
Charlotte Lamb

Magic of the Baobab
Yvonne Whittal

Available from July 1991. Price: £6.40

Available from Boots, Martins, John Menzies, W.H. Smith, Woolworths
and other paperback stockists.

Also available from Mills and Boon Reader Service,
P.O. Box 236, Thornton Road, Croydon, Surrey CR9 3RU.